In Support of Black Lives

First Edition August 2020

Dedicated to all victims of racism and discrimination.

Table of Contents:

Introduction...4

About the Charities...................................6

About the Writing...................................8

Meet the Contributors..........................9

Part 1...18

Part 2...86

Conclusion...122

Helplines..125

Resources...134

Introduction:

How This Anthology Came About:

On May 25th 2020, a man was murdered by the Minneapolis police. Millions of people saw the murder of George Floyd captured on video and while many found it shocking, for more it was not a surprise; but an unpleasant reliving of an experience they'd had countless times before.

Within days, protests were organised across the United States, and soon across the world. This was in the midst of a global pandemic where not attending public gatherings was considered paramount to public health and safety. Yet, the signs many people carried told the truth:

RACISM IS A PANDEMIC.

Statues were toppled, petitions signed, politicians sidestepped valid questions about institutional racism almost as if it was their day job. Racism became a trending topic across social media, and like it or not, the entire world was talking about it. Suddenly everyone and their casually racist grandpa was on the street, either tearing down a statue of a slave owner or fighting to keep it up. Books about race and colonialism were flung between friends and strangers at a dizzying rate, Netflix added a new genre to their list: Black Lives Matter. The height of the protests was a time of extreme chaotic and strangely hopeful feelings. When the world is up in smoke, what will rise from the ashes?

Like most people as they watched the United States burn, police brutality unfolding on countless innocent protesters, and conservative governments refuse to acknowledge the current issues of racism, I felt helpless. Outraged, uncomprehending of how deep-seated racism is not just in the United States, but around the world. As a broke student scrabbling for a job in the midst of a crumbling economy, I wasn't sure what to do, aside from educating myself on the issues of racism, internal and institutional.

A cursory conversation with friends and family told me everyone was feeling the same, but nobody was quite sure how to cope with it. My degree in Literature and Creative Writing certainly didn't seem like it was going to be helpful, but I decided to do my best with what I had at home: my writing and an internet connection (therefore a worldwide connection).

Every contributor in this anthology is a volunteer. Many of us didn't know each other before I put out the call for submissions for this anthology over social media (turns out mum was wrong: talking to strangers on the internet does sometimes do you good). Everyone put their hard work and artistic talent into their submissions for the greater good, to make a difference. Everyone's had to deal with a lot of pestering emails from me, and undoubtedly a lot of work on their own amazing entries even without my micromanaging eye. Thank you, everyone!

About the Charities:

Every penny from this anthology is going to charity. Two charities, to be exact:

<u>THE NATIONAL BAIL FUND NETWORK</u>

(www.communityjusticeexchange.org/nbfn-directory)

This is a network of over sixty community bail funds across the United States. Their work is not localised to paying bail/bond, but also fighting to abolish the money bail system and pretrial detention, as well as immigration detention.

Their work is especially vital right now, as the COVID-19 Pandemic has turned many prisons and jails into hot spots for the virus. During the Pandemic, they are fighting to release those detained who can and should be freed under the current money bail system, as a way of flattening the curve and keeping people safer and healthier than they would be behind bars.

Much of how the United States legal system will treat you is tied not only to your race and social position, but also to your income. The National Bail Fund Network is a sort of pool of money between communities to help fight multiple drivers of criminalisation and incarceration from the bottom up, such as court fees, fines, probation/parole, etc...

<u>KNOW YOUR RIGHTS CAMP</u>

(www.knowyourrightscamp.com)

In addition to doing a TON of work helping Black and Brown communities throughout the pandemic, Know Your

Rights Camp is an educational experience providing vital information to young minorities. The initiative began as a way to teach young people how to handle encounters with law enforcement, and expanded to giving young people the resources, access, and knowledge to brighten their futures.

These conversations are a vital education, and yet they aren't the kinds of things you'll find in schools: what do you do if you're pulled over by a police officer? What are your rights? Camp educates, empowers, and mobilises the next generation of Black and Brown leaders. If we want the world to change for the better, we need to be investing in things like this.

Additionally, their Legal Defense Initiative has connections with top defense lawyers and Civil Rights lawyers across the United States to provide much-needed legal resources to people and communities suffering from injustice and police brutality.

About the Writing:

Many of the writers didn't feel comfortable discussing racism within our writing, even as we wanted to contribute to the cause.

As such, the anthology is split into two parts: Part One, which is full of writing and art dedicated to current events and anti-racism; and Part Two, which contains more general writing. This is also done on behalf of readers who may not want to risk awakening their own racial trauma and those who perhaps want a lighter read when they pick up this book. If Part 1 ever gets too heavy for you, check out a poem or short story from Part 2!

While it is important we continue to educate ourselves throughout these turbulent times, it is important to take a deep breath when things get too intense. Some of our stories, as in real life, contain unsavoury, prejudiced characters that do not represent the views of the authors, but are in place to encourage thought and conversation in the real world. This can be an intense experience, and it is important not to push yourself too far too fast. In the Resources section at the back of this anthology are a number of helplines and websites you can access if you find yourself struggling with mental health or racial issues.

Without further ado, please enjoy this anthology!

Meet the Contributors:

Imane Chafi- Writer

I am a Software Engineering student at McGill University. When I'm not helping design rocketry structures with the school's rocket team, you can find me painting, reading, and enjoying a warm cup of hot chocolate on rainy days. As the EUS Publications Director, I oversee and engage in writing articles to promote the arts, and make sure that the engineering newspapers always provide quality content for the students to enjoy.

Alice Challoner- Cover Artist

Alice is the name, and respectfully agreeing from a distance is MY game. Since drawing from a young age, I've had lots of practice, and am extremely grateful to be given the opportunity to put my trade into promoting a movement as important and revolutionary as Black Lives Matter. As someone who drinks up pop culture like I'm severely dehydrated, it'd be unjust to ignore the massive contributions Black people have made to western culture, in particular, Black trans women. Silence is violence, and to ignore an entire group of people who have tirelessly shown time and time again that they are more than deserving of equal treatment is obviously sickening. As a message to fellow whiteys; remember to read your history, educate yourselves, and listen to Black and Indigenous folks. If you'd like to find me on social media, my instagram is **@alices.fresh.doodles**. Thank you for reading, and BLM!

S. Collins (@litlangislife)- Writer, Editor

Like most people when they watched the murder of George Floyd, I was outraged, terrified, and uncomprehending of how something like this could be happening again. I wanted to do something bigger than social media or signing petitions, but I had no idea what. I was a broke student trying to find a job in the middle of a global pandemic and now a long-approaching cultural revolution. After taking some time to educate myself and really think about what I could do, I decided to start this project and put the skills I learned in my degree to good use.

Victoria Croft - Writer

So, I used to hate metaphors. Really hate them. Which is weird for a poet. I don't know, they always remind me of the poems you study in school where the teacher has to explain everything or it has to be explained on the opposite page Shakespeare-style before you can understand what it says. I like poems that are simple. The ones where you just read and feel, without having to analyse.

But I've always been intrigued by metaphors. I always wondered if the poet actually mean to mean any of that, or if academics just added the meaning in afterwards. So I've been trying to use more metaphors. My life's aim is to write a poem that looks like it's bursting with meaning and metaphors, but in really it doesn't mean anything. It's complete nonsense.

But that poem isn't done yet. Instead, here's a poem, with a metaphor. I also love a good twist, so have one of those too.

Milicent Fambrough- Writer

I am an artist firstly having been encouraged and influenced by family to create at an early stage in life. I became a avid writer second. This was also seen by family as a talent and of course being encouraged to write frequently. I did these things for enjoyment and didn't realize their value until much later. Now as an adult with a college education I see the value of both artistic expression and the pleasure of writing. I have found my voice in both. I still encourage others to create all the time.

I feel having a voice and exercising it has worth. This particularly why I would love to contribute to publications. That and something about leading by example or something to that affect.

Jess Goode- Writer

As soon as I heard about this opportunity I wanted to contribute. I cannot say I know a lot about Black history, but since George Floyd's murder made global news, I knew something had to change. Admittedly I felt uncomfortable reading about it, but I've been reading the likes of *The Bluest Eye*, *Becoming*, and *Girl, Woman, Other*, and watching documentaries such as 13th on Netflix in an attempt to educate myself. Although tentative at first,

writing has given me the chance to explore my feelings on the surrounding subjects, which I've been exploring to some extent on my blog too:
https://therunningequestrian.sport.blog/ Hopefully by engaging with my own feelings and learning about the subject through literature, we can encourage others to do the same.

Ava Greene- Writer

As a white American woman, I've never felt right writing about race. It's just not my ball-park, and while I have tried before, that doesn't seem like my place in the BLM movement. I prefer to step back and listen whenever I can to marginalised voices, rather than speak for them. Still, when I heard about this project, I wanted to contribute something more than a 'share' or 'like'. Racism is not and never has been just a social media trend- it's something we need to actively fight, on-screen and off.

Celia Hameury- Writer

I am an engineering student who loves to write. Having spent the early years of my life in Montreal, Canada, I later traveled around the world on a sailboat with my family. It is this experience which first inspired me to begin writing. In my spare time, I also enjoy working with clay and reading. I was eager to participate in this anthology for the **#BLM** movement because I believe it is a noble cause and wanted to contribute.

Brian Judge- Artist

I'm Brian Judge. I'm a cartoonist located out in North Carolina. I love making comix and post nearly everything I make on my Instagram (**@one_and_only_comics**)! If you liked what you see, I've also got an online store too with exclusive material for each of my comics (**oneandonlycomics.bigcartel.com**)! I made 'Lonely Earth' as a way of expressing my own thoughts and feelings towards the topic of police brutality in America. I believe that stories have the power to promote cultural ideals and that they can be provide a vision for how the future can be. I wanted to make a story that didn't stray away from showing the imperfections of the world but still had a message of hope for the future. I think that hope is a powerful tool and that no matter what problems we face in the world today, we are still able to strive for a better tomorrow.

Kish Sofia

I have been creatively writing for many years as a hobby that is the fuel to my soul. I exist, so I write and vice versa. That is the infinity loop that is within me. My educational background is in Chemical Engineering and I have worked in corporate leadership for over a decade.

I grew up in many parts of the world due to my father's work and some people refer to us as "Global Nomads" or TCK Adults ("Third Culture Kids" as Adults). I was 1 year old when my parents left their native land and by the time I turned 20 years old, I had lived in 3 continents, 6 countries, 8 cities and went to 8 different schools.

I am a lover of the ocean, poetry, hot summers, art, music and lots of delicious food from all around the world. And above it all, I am a seeker of truth and liberation for all of humanity.

I am part of the BIPOC (Black, Indigenous, People of Colour) group with both Brown and Indigenous roots. I am passionate about both #blacklivesmatter and #indigenouslivesmatter movements. I am a single mother of a little girl who visually identifies as White and we have many interesting and painful discussions on the current state of the world. I believe it is only with open dialogue with each other that we can attempt to heal and help shape our children's mind, our future.

D. Relm- Writer and Essayist

I've never been particularly interested in racism or the history of it until I saw the murder of George Floyd, and the subsequent explosion of the world. It really brought home to me how apathetic my life had been up until that point, whether it was a lack of education at home, at school, or by knowing few minority people in real life. I realise now it was a veil of ignorance that shrouded my entire life, and that potentially put other people at risk just for existing. I have been educating myself ever since, trying to become a better person and using my writing skills to disseminate the information I've learned in an easily digestible format. Never again will I be silent when a family member says something not-so-secretly racist. I hope by contributing to this anthology we can send a message to all those who proclaim it is enough to be non-racist. It isn't- we must be vehemently, enthusiastically, ceaselessly, anti-racist.

Liz Rivers- Writer

My poetry usually stays far away from politics, but racism isn't politics; it's a human rights issue, not a matter of who you vote for. I was lucky to be raised in America and in Columbia. In America, I was another white face and part of the majority. In Columbia, that changed, and suddenly my white skin marked me as 'other'. Upon moving back to the U.S., I had a new understanding of what it is like to feel marginalized. I know I can never wash the privilege from my skin, but using my privilege and understanding together as part of projects like this is what I live for.

Qasim Shan- Writer

I never wanted to write, but because of who I am, or more specifically what I am, I felt a need to do so. It was a gnawing and inescapable urge to tell the world of my experiences, no matter how mundane they felt to me. Once I began writing about my experiences as an ethnic minority in the contemporary world, I realised what I had been repressing all this time; a life of pain, anguish and heartache. Writing about my own life has become somewhat of a revelation, and it is in this endeavour whereupon I found a passion for the truth of the person I am, and the heritage I am proud to cherish.

My name is Qasim Shan, and I am a writer.

J.R.R. Stewart- Essayist

I'm a Physics and Astrophysics student at the university of Dundee. I know this doesn't exactly sound like the type of person to be writing an essay in an anthology, but I feel that this is important. I was very surprised to find out that many people my age never learnt about the long and bloody history of racism in the US throughout the 20th and 21s centuries, so, with some prompting, I managed to contribute something.

Cassandra Temple- Writer

One of the greatest questions I often ask myself is 'What is magic'? Is it turning people into frogs? It is miraculously curing the sick? Or is it just a feeling? A secret power that only you can feel?

There's a certain magic in words. After all, there's a reason why so many spells rhyme. I've always greatly enjoyed rhyming. My teacher at primary school always used to lecture me that not all poetry had to rhyme. Well, I delight in rhyme. So, take that.

But, I digress. One thing I have noticed in recent years is how the label Witch is used in modern society. There has been a rise in Neopagan beliefs and a rise in people reclaiming the word with a sense of pride. Yet there are still so many people for whom 'Witch' simply means nasty or manipulative woman. This version of witch is often used when the woman is correct. Thus, I was intrigued when President Trump insisted on using 'witch-hunt' to describe seemingly anyone who disagreed with him. Almost to depict him, a good, upstanding man, as being attacked by the mean, nasty leftists. Which, ironically seemed to ignore that there were a lot of 'good' and 'upstanding' people who led witch-hunts and burned, stoned or drowned so many. As I mused upon the changing use of witch hunt, this poem was born.

I hope that you take delight in this during these difficult times. And if you happen to find a certain magic or power in my rhymes, I hope you carry it with you.

Ruth Thompson- Writer

My name is Ruth Thompson and I am an avid writer. I decided to contribute to this anthology to spread awareness on racism and how it can be integrated into someone through primary socialisation, through another's attitudes, or just simply being around it. I wanted to show how the victim feels as that isn't always shown, yet also show how racism isn't always open, it can be subtle. My piece is a hybrid of poetry and prose which I chose to do to add emotional depth to the characters and to give a more chilling account of the struggles the victim goes through.

PART 1

Change

By Imane Chafi

I wake up every morning

Asking myself why

Why the hurt, why the racism

Keeps happening and reappearing

Incessantly, like the ticks of a clock

The cold freezing water

Of a fear of our protectors,

Our police and benefactors

Keeps flowing and resurfacing

Drowning any hopes of security

Any hopes of safety

Too many times, lives were lost

Too many times, for reasons lost

Too many times, humanities lost

And for what? A lost anger?

A horrid dark rage you couldn't contain?

What made you commit a crime

So vile and futile

Your own humanity was lost?

This cannot, will not stand

Not in a world where we live and breathe

As inevitable as the storm after lightning

Change is coming

SPACE AND TIME

By Imane Chafi

As the silent darkness drifts upon our heads

We follow the flickering light that shines ahead

And the way it moves and changes directions

To send a message to those who need protection

These are wicked times and wicked lines,

And as I see the world bring itself to the ground

I look at the sky and hope to see the night's sign

That humans will one day come around

And understand that mindless fights for frightening and jealousy

Only brings with it the heavy dread of a felony

I look back at the sky to understand what fuels their rage

But I only see the obscenity of a grey and purple cage

Bombs and weapons won't bring satisfaction

For the need for more needs is the curse of those people

And the small particles that were made from attraction

Sometimes fall from the sky to remind us that we are all
equal

The Secret

By S. Collins

Age 4. Bishakha (Bisha, because my mouth can't form her name) is my best friend, but Beth is prettier so I cling close to her and her blonde hair and her Barbie-blue eyes. God, she's gorgeous.

In school we learn Adam and Eve. God was white, Adam and Eve were white and there was the Serpent, opposite of all good and white so I guess he must be Black. In school we watch Disney's Jim Crows but never learn about our own because children are too young to know about that kind of thing, you know.

But Bisha knows. I ask her about her brown skin one day and her eyes fill with tears, big brown eyes with thick lashes and thicker brows. *It's such a shame such a big shame* she says before her mother calls us inside because if we burn she'll get browner and we can't have that.

I turn princess-pink in the sun but that doesn't stop me from having fun and by the time I'm six my face is a field of freckles everywhere, even on my eyelids. I wonder why mum doesn't stop me going into the sun, because one day all my freckles will melt together and I'll be brown like Bisha and that must be bad, right?

Mum tells me we're all created equal, never say the bad words to people like Bisha, never remind them of their colour. She buys books and movies and tells stories of the times grandma told her,

Don't marry a Black man, you'll have a Black baby.

And she tells me,

'I'd love you just as much if you were Black, brown, or gay.'

'Gray,' I correct her. She leaves that conversation for later. No room for rainbows in her Black and White words.

Seven years old, moving to an orange island in a Caribbean-blue sea, and nobody here is anything but white. Apart from the security guard, but he's scary. He looks at me every day as I head out to school and play, and once I heard him behind me while I was bent over a water fountain and I didn't swallow didn't do anything but run and look over my shoulder to see him, frowning and thirsty.

New friends move here, and they don't speak my language, but it's okay. I don't speak theirs either. We communicate in a series of grunts and groans, pointing at pretty rocks on the beach and collecting shells together. Two boys and one girl, who turn into two brothers and one sister.

I'm not in England when Grandma dies, but they're here with me, they don't know what's gone on but they know something's wrong and for a week they give me all the best seashells until life is normal again. I wonder if grandma would hate them, because their father is white and their mother isn't. I wonder if she'd hate me too, because they are my family now.

Big Brother has muscles that will only become more defined while we grow up, but for now I'm seven and don't care about those kinds of things, only know that I will one day so it's best to keep an eye out. When we grow up

I'll make sure he knows his worth to other girls and doesn't settle for less.

Little Brother cries a lot. Once he fell from the front of a dinghy and was nearly cut to pieces in the propeller. I saw from the land as he was sucked under, my eyes glued to the white froth behind the boat, waiting for a splash of red as his Father stopped it spinning and his Mother screamed, only for his head to come up from the water with a big beaming grin like he'd just met God.

Sister reminds me of Bisha. Same quiet sadness so uncommon in children, unless they know The Secret. I don't find out The Secret for several silent years so for now I marvel in every curl of her hair and the depths of her brown eyes, like finding an old friend all over again.

Dad works on our home in the sun, on the deck, pulling engine pieces out and putting them back in again while mum sews the sails until we're ready, and we sail, and I never see my Brothers or Sister again. This is a recurring theme with my family.

I don't see anyone again, not for a long time, not until I open my eyes and all at once I'm eleven years old. We're in Columbia, a whole other world, for the first time. It's the first time I'm the tallest in every room and nobody, *nobody* looks like me or my family, sticking out like the first drop of snow on the sidewalk, ready to be trod on, because *Gabachos* don't know how to haggle. We don't speak the language. We live here, but we're just tourists, because we look like tourists.

Here, I begin to learn The Secret. It starts when a group of girls come up to us with a camera.

'Never seen so much white!' We make out between our broken Spanish and their broken English.

I smile and wonder when I became a commodity. Little do I know what others have been through.

Walking home, we take a wrong turn and suddenly none of the buildings have paint on them and chickens cluck in the street running from men with machetes who stop when they see us and I know that look that hungry look and all of a sudden my skin isn't a commodity it's *comida* or a curse as I clutch my purse and let dad lead us safely back to sea.

Later, we see a museum. Inside is the worst of mankind- tongs, pikes, knives, devices with no name but the blackened metal of which has been cleaned of countless lives. Our guide laughs as he tells us the trauma our country caused: the robbing, raping, relapsing hatred held for those we found here, hundreds of years ago, for those we robbed of glistening red gold and kept in human zoos back home in Europe, where I've never lived but always called home... but how can home be so barbaric?

My ancestors built castles and forts here, but today I sit on the deck of my own home, my own castle, with the ocean for a moat, watching the sun set on a city my ancestors simultaneously burned and built. I feel the guilt of a thousand guilts burrowing deep inside me and think back to that day in Bisha's back yard, where I saw The Secret in her eyes, and I want to scrape the privilege, the genocide, the bad blood from my skin. But when it's the skin you're in you can't help it, so instead I lie back on deck watching the anchor go from taut to slack and back until the sky goes black.

Panama City, Panama. I'm twelve here, and I never leave, not really. I find a home here, metropolitan expats and Kuna Abuelas selling *molas* and stinking sailors like myself. I learn to make and sell jewelry and barter like the best abuela: *Two necklaces for one mola. Last offer. I'm going home. Alright, sold!*

But I have a taste of The Secret, and whenever I walk through the mall, the only one stood too tall even when I'm slouching and all, I just want to look like everyone else. I want the black hair, the tanned skin, I don't want to be a *gabacha* for the rest of my life.

'Gringos.' Slurs some drunk patriot in Peru, propped up between two friends as I walk by with my family. I am a *gringa*, I can handle that. But he makes the slashing motion across his throat and his look is death so I walk just a little bit faster to get home, hiding below deck just in case he saw where we live. I count the gunshots outside but don't dare put my head near a hatch.

'I know you're not from here,' Smiles the man who owns the marina. By now I speak Spanish enough to know what he means, but I'd know even without the words. 'I can tell from the way you walk, the way you talk, the way you carry yourself.'

And he's right- I'm the Briton who's never lived in Britain.

When I'm fourteen we turn back to Britain and I think, *I will never be a gabacha again.*

Everyone here is tall, burly, blonde and with eyes Barbie-blue like me, like Beth, and I've never been more scared in my life. Everyone here speaks with a fascism louder than any I've heard before, telling me the score:

'If you're from South America, why aren't you Black?'

'Are you one of those white Asians?'

Nobody here can place me, and so here I am, a *gabacha* once again.

'Are you white?'

'Yes.'

'There's something... ethnic about you.'

I wait for someone to tell me they can tell I'm not from here, to tell me it's in the way I dress or walk or talk, something I can fix, but they can never pinpoint *what it is*. Some of them smile their well-meaning smiles like they don't know what it is to be racist and they say,

'It's cool. I don't see colour.'

Which is strange, because that's *all* I see. It's all I've felt: my white privilege, our white privilege, a disdain for whiteness, the miracle of being white, of having ancestors who killed, raped, murdered and justified themselves with the whip or the cross. The curse of *being* a curse for countless cultures.

Americans I used to know wave the confederate flag to celebrate their ancestors and I can't help but think *What for? Are you proud your ancestors owned, humiliated, destroyed people?* There were supposed to be ten plagues, but we were the final one to befall Egypt; sweeping across the globe stealing gold and crops and people and crystals and cultures. When we took slaves, we didn't let them go either. I wonder what Great-Great-Grandma made of Moses. Did she side with Pharaoh?

I meet older friends for the first time at fifteen, one just rejoined from being deployed and I can't help but wonder if he loves his country enough, sipping British beer in a British garden and wishing he could take a bullet for the Queen he has never met.

Later, when I write about Black Lives Matter, he will reply asking if I really believe it, when #alllivesmatter, and the only thing I have trouble believing is that he's from the same planet.

I learn more about The Secret the more time I spend with my pale British friends, until I've all-but forgotten the sting of that word, *Gringo*. Eventually my eyes stop searching for other Latin people because I realise: I'm not one of them. But I sit with my white friends as they talk about how hot the Black girls are because *'they're all thick chicks looking for dicks'* and I know I can't really be sat here listening to whatever this is eating my lunch with people who look like me but who aren't me, who can't be me.

There is no training you can do to defend yourself from The Secret, not at first. It crashed down on me in a memory of Bishakha's *Bharatanatyam* performance with her stage clothes all blue and gold and smile painted onto her face and to me she looked like divinity but to those who know the words to her song she looked like home, home they'd left to come to the land of the free, land of opportunity.

Too young to realise I wasn't one of them, the glittery gold of her performance danced across my mind, her bare brown feet twirling tilting swirling. Beauty, grace, face grinning telling a story all its own and her hands heavy with henna.

Her house was a whole other world. A thousand scents I didn't learn words for until much later, but I knew I never smelled such spices outside. These performances that gathered so many people like her parents, immigrants with American children born with another piece of them in a land they'd never known.

Mum and Me there too, outsiders for sure but not in a bubble of whiteness like we are now, in Britain. What happens when you are an immigrant in your home country? What happens when you know racism in every way- outward, inward, institutional, familial?

The Secret of Racism is so blatant you know you've known your whole life, but it doesn't dawn on you until you're seeing it on screens in memes and everywhere in front of you outside. And you know you're on the guilty side, even if you're a *gabacha* you are also a *gringa, guera*, privilege painted over your face but this paint doesn't wash away.

Family know there's something wrong with me but it's nothing a trip to the pub can't handle. I bring a notebook, because it's the only place that feels real anymore. This is deeper than a pint glass, but I down a few anyway, because 'I'm British' and if I don't they'll *know*.

Pub screens flicker a moment and it takes me more to slur the words together in my mind:

BLACK MAN KILLED BY POLICE

I CAN'T BREATHE

FATHER OF THREE

LAND OF THE FREE?

BLACK LIVES MATTER PROTESTS

RIOTERS BURN

'All lives matter,' scoffs someone I share DNA with.

STATUES TORN DOWN

'He was a hero,' agrees another. 'Men like that made this country.'

I think of the slavery museum across the Atlantic. It had a replica of a holding cell where you stand and you feel the invisible bodies that built our whole white world for real and you know, you *know*...

I know The Secret intimately by the time I wake up next and I'm twenty, and it's happened again.

Again.

Another father doing the normal thing at the normal time taken down by normal officers, and it's totally normal. The fire in my throat has become normal. The guilt with no action, just listening to my loved ones lamenting *it's all bullshit* and knowing I'm not one of them, either. I'm white enough to be the oppressor, but I've felt eyes on me, judging me, knowing a wrong idea of me from my colour. But here I am, silent, the oppressor.

Tired of the guilt with no action. Tired of the burn in my throat from the words stuck there like, 'He wasn't a hero, he was a war criminal, slave owner, racist' and 'How can all lives matter when *His* life didn't?'

But *He* is the final straw that explodes across not only the news but into protests on every street and all over social media that unsticks the words from the back of my teeth as I scream: NO MORE.

NO MORE

NO MORE

NO MORE

My story has no end, only resentment that refuses to be quiet for another second. Only understanding that demands to be put in writing right now, right this second. I refuse to be part of the problem any longer. Silence is violence. Guilt is useless unless we **all** recognise ours. I have been racist. I have learned. I have had race used against me. I have learned. I will keep learning.

No more Secrets.

My Friend Marley

By S. Collins

Marley blames me. I know it wasn't my fault, but I guess to him it was. I always knew Marley wasn't a 'thug', but now I don't know what he is, or how he is. The people who keep spreading rumours about him should be ashamed of themselves. I need to tell someone about what really happened at the party, because all the lies are still floating around in my head. Maybe, if I get down what really happened, I'll finally be able to stop thinking about it.

Exams were in full thrust. We'd got out of school early. My head hurt from all the maths, and Marley was smiling because he knew already he'd done well. I was struck by his relaxed shoulders and quiet smile, basking in the afterglow of school. Exams were his element, not mine.

Our arms linked, his dark skin contrasting the white of mine. My brain started to loosen up from the exam tension, still spaced out from staring at trigonometry for too long. I skipped because no one was around to watch me, a sixteen-year-old, acting like a six-year-old. I dragged Marley along at my pace.

'I got a text from my mate, Sam,' I said, ignoring the way my head pounded when it had to do anything too strenuous, like come up with words.

'Who?'

'Sam- you know, the guy who goes to uni, in town?' Marley's face was a mildly hesitant mask.

I grinned and hoped I looked enticing. 'He's invited me to a party tonight. I don't want to go on my own, so I was hoping... Maybe, you would...?'

Eyes widening, Marley's arm stiffened around mine. 'My mum would kill me.'

'Don't be a pussy, Marl. Y'know, we both need to lighten up before the biology exam. We have a whole weekend to worry about that. Can't we just... cut loose, tonight?'

I knew he wouldn't disappoint me- Marley never disappointed anybody. He was just about the nicest kid you could expect to come out of the worse side of town. It wasn't exactly Harlem, but it wasn't the Hamptons. Half the kids from his neighbourhood would grow up to be menial labourers or just arrested seemingly for being alive. All noble professions, but Marley looked at the workers and 'thug-types' around him with a thin veneer of acceptance. None of them seemed to notice he never once reached for the alcohol, made an excuse whenever someone tried to pass him a spliff, and hardly did anything social without being dragged kicking and screaming into it… usually by me.

He wanted more, so much more than a quick buck or a cheap high. He wanted a six-figure salary- a prestigious job, like a lawyer or a politician. He'd rise up the ranks like a tsunami, and nothing would stop him from doing his best. Wanting to help people, that was Marley. And he was on the fast track to getting there.

Marley sighed before he inevitably relented. 'Fine, Mel. But if we get into trouble and fail our exams, I'm becoming an alcoholic on your couch, y'hear?'

'I hear. Thanks, Marl. We're gonna have such a great time!' I resumed our skipping pace and tried not to notice how the smile on Marley's face had shrunk as we went along.

We parted ways at the bus stop. Hugging Marley, I told him: 'Eight 'o clock. Meet me back here right on time, mister!'

Then he got on board, and I didn't.

I was an explosive embodiment of caffeinated bliss as party-time drew closer. My first real party! High school parties couldn't possibly be anything like university ones! Those were kid parties, but this was an adult party, and so I wore my most adult clothes- a short black dress and knee-high boots. I painted neon-blue eyeliner on until I looked like Cleopatra's little sister, but too pale to be an Egyptian. My thighs looked like uncooked fish fingers, but I shook the insecurity away. *Adults are confident. Adults go out and have a good time, and we're gonna have a* great *time tonight.*

I told my parents I was going to see a school play Marley was acting in, and they believed me. I wish I hadn't lied to them.

Marley met me at the bus stop and after a short ride we walked through the cool summer night to the university campus. From there it was pretty easy to find the block of flats where Sam lived, because they were the only ones with blaring music. It sounded like every flat was having a party, and my heart sped up in my chest. The music swelled, and the beat echoed in my pulse as it reverberated through the ground. This was it. The night Marley and I would remember- hanging out with cool people. Maybe one of us would meet the love of our life at this party, or we'd hook up with someone and have reckless casual sex, like on telly.

I bit my lip, took a deep breath, and tried not to get ahead of myself. It'd be nice to just drink irresponsibly and make out with somebody.

Still linked with mine, I could feel Marley's arm shaking. He was dressed conservatively, with white sneakers, plain jeans and a grey hoodie. Eyes focused straight ahead, looking as if he wanted to melt into the blackness of the night, as though he had no right being there. I shook his arm and grinned.

'Hey, lighten up. Nobody here wants to shoot you. We're just here to have a good time.'

Marley forced a smile, raising his eyebrows just to make sure I knew he was forcing it. He was still shaking. 'How are you never nervous about anything?'

'How are you nervous about *everything?*' I countered, nudging him with my elbow.

'The counselor says it's because of how it was in primary school, back in Kent.'

I looked at my feet as we ascended the three flights of stairs to get to Sam's, suddenly silent. Marley had been the only Black kid in school. Kids are cruel. He didn't have to fill in any blanks on why his family had moved farther North.

'Mel! ...Mel's friend! Come on in!' Sam flicked his long hair out of his eyes as he ushered us inside.

'Great to see ya! Grab a drink, everything's on the table. Drink the orange stuff at your own risk, though.'

I smelled the orange stuff before I spotted it on the table- it was something artificial and something alcoholic.

Marley grabbed a cup and poured water from the tap, eyes darting around behind his glasses as though all the older kids were about to rip his head off.

I poured myself a cup of the orange stuff. *What's life without a few bad decisions?* I headed over to Marley and nudged him again, grinning.

'It's not a funeral, we're allowed to have some fun.'

'I am having fun,' He tried to joke. 'This is *unfiltered* tap water.'

'Ooooh, living life on the dangerous side. But how about...' I took his cup and handed him mine. 'You let me do the worrying for tonight?'

His eyes were doubtful, but he took a sip anyway. His face turned sour. 'What is that?'

I chortled. 'Fucked if I know.'

'Ah.' He took another sip, tilting his head back so that it all went down his throat- the world's biggest shot. His face looked like he'd just swallowed bitter cough medicine. 'Cool.'

We eventually found an empty couch. Marley had stopped trembling, but his dark eyes were still darting from person to person, like a fish that's been dragged out of water and is just beginning to suffocate. I could tell his anxiety was getting the better of him. *Fuck, why can't he just relax?*

'Marl?' I tried to look him in the face. I hoped he was listening. 'You okay?'

'I think the booze is taking hold.'

'That's good. You might loosen up a little.'

'I hope I do. I don't feel... loose.'

I was about to suggest we go home when someone came over and sat next to us. He was lanky and long dreadlocks fell around his pale face. With his loose clothes, pierced everything, and unshaven face, he looked like the ultimate hippie.

'Sup, guys? Cool party, huh?'

'Y-yeah.' Marley couldn't look at him. 'Great party.'

'You alright, li'l man? You don't look so fine.'

'He's just had a bit to drink.' I smiled, trying to take the heat off Marley. Hippy Guy fist-bumped my extended hand before he shook it. 'I'm Mel, this is Marley.'

'Mel and Marl, huh? Cool stuff. I'm Funko.'

'Funko?'

'Yeah. I decided to pick a name more suited to me and my belief system.' He leaned in closer to us as he whispered, 'I'm actually 5% Black and 25% Asian. My ancestors came to this country on a slave ship. Fucking disgraceful.'

'Did they?' Marley's voice had an edge to it I couldn't identify. 'That's nice.'

'It's the fucking opposite of nice- you oughta know, my brown-brother.' Funko squinted at Marley for a moment, and I saw how blown his pupils were. 'Hey, brother, you look tense. You wanna try some weed?'

'No thanks.'

'How about you, li'l sister?' He produced a spliff from his pocket, lit it, and offered it to me.

Fuck it, I thought. *It's a party. It's an experience.*

I took it from his hands, held it up close to my lips, and inhaled.

'Hold the smoke in your lungs, long as you can.' Funko seemed to intuitively know I'd never smoked anything before in my life. I spluttered everything out after five seconds and he took a drag before handing it back to me.

His big eyes focused in on Marley, who was watching us and had his hands clasped together tightly, lips knit into a tight line. 'What's your deal, li'l brother? Why don't you like this stuff?'

'I just don't.' Marley murmured.

'You had a bad experience? I've seen you 'round my old neighbourhood. Guys from there'll sell you anything for a bit of green. This stuff isn't like that. My mom grows this shit herself.'

'I've never tried it.'

Funko fixed Marley with a stare. 'How's someone like you lived in that boring-ass cul-de-sac and never smoked a joint to roll the edge off?' Funko started to giggle before Marley could answer.

I didn't think I felt any different, until I realised I was giggling too, and holding the joint. I passed it back to Funko, who blew the smoke in Marley's direction.

'You know, li'l brother, this is a part of our heritage? Yeah, the white man wanted a chance to deport the

Mexicans and hold down the Blacks, so he decided, 'Yeah, we should criminalise marijuana, and since it's mainly them People of Colour selling it, we're basically criminalising them, too. They'll fuck off back to Mexico in no time." He broke into hysterical giggling. 'God told us to partake of the herb, you know that, li'l brown-brother?'

'I don't go to church.'

'Who said anything about church? I'm talking about *real* religion. I'm talking about *feeling* God right down, *deep* in your bones- breathing in *God...*' At this point he took a deep breath from the spliff, he exhaled, 'And breathing him right out again. Li'l brother, it's magical. You oughta try it. It'd make you feel better.' Funko chuckled a bit more before continuing, while I was entranced and giggling at random intervals because of how funny words suddenly sounded. 'In the 60s, they were testing this on people with anxiety, depression- everything wrong with ya. Then good old Uncle Sam decided to make everything illegal. Now nobody's talking about it anymore. It's a fucking travesty, man.'

Funko seemed to have forgotten the catalyst of his rant- that Marley wasn't up for smoking- as he handed the last remnants of the spliff to Marley. Marley had apparently had a change of heart, and held it up to his lips, just as the door burst open.

'Alright everyone, party's over!'

An officer came into the apartment, followed by two more. I felt Marley stiffen as he put the spliff out on the table before they could see it. I stared at the black hole it left on the wood and tried not to cackle like a hyena. Everything was unreasonably funny. My cheeks dimpled themselves in a Cheshire cat grin, but I kept my lips shut. *If they can't see your teeth, you aren't reeeeallly smiling.*

As the officers moved to turn the stereo off, Funko took a massive bag of weed out of his pocket and pushed it into Marley's hands. His once-relaxed voice sounded frantic; terrified.

'In case they search us. I got priors, man! I can't go to jail! You're just a kid. They'll let you off with a warning and everything will be just fine.'

Marley's eyes were wide and he'd started shaking again as he stuffed the weed into his pocket. *Marley, you fucking idiot drunk!*

One of the cops was sniffing deeply, and my heart stopped as I realised what he was thinking. *Oh, fuck.*

'Alright,' he said. 'Who here's got the pot?'

The stereo was off. The whole room was silent. The head officer sighed and pointed to the wall. 'Everybody line up against there, if nobody's owning up to it then we're going to have to search you all individually.'

I squeezed Marley's hand and tried to give him my 'it's-going-to-be-fine' look, but he was already hyperventilating. Maybe if I hadn't had that spliff, or maybe if he hadn't been drinking, we could have just put the weed under the table, or under the couch, or anywhere not on us. We would have been fine.

But the look Marley gave me... He was pissed. And terrified. I could read his mind: *'I'm a Black teenager at a party with a bushel of weed in my pocket. How well do you think this is going to go for me?'* Or maybe it was just an annoyed look, and I was just high. Fuck, I was so high. Not just the giggly kind- it was starting to be a new, paranoid kind of high, like the clacking of a rollercoaster as it ascends.

We were the last to line up, and the nearest to the window. Outside, you could see the fire escape. The closer the officers got to us, the more I could feel Marley shake. My heart was beating out of my chest. We could make a run for it. We could get away.

Then, my brain short-circuited. I started laughing. I don't even know at what now, and I doubt I even knew then either. Marley shot me a look, a subliminal message: *Shut the fuck up, what the fuck are you doing?* Funko started giggling, too, on the opposite side of Marley. His giggle sounded like a happy baby, and it made me laugh harder. I could feel the other people at the party staring at us, but I was learning a terrible truth: it didn't matter, because I was having a good time. One officer came over to us three and waved flashlights in our faces.

'We got some pie-eyes over here, Fred,' said one officer.

'Aw, shit. I coulda told you that.' replied a giggling Funko.

'One of you got something for us to confiscate?'

'Me? Officer, never!' Funko was stuck in the happiness like a fly in amber.

'Turn out your pockets.' Funko and I did as we were told, while Marley stood, frozen.

'Son, we have a warrant to search this property and anyone on it. Turn out your pockets.'

I knew Sam was shady, but not officers-on-his-doorstep-armed-with-warrants shady. The surprise and the sudden gravity of the situation made me giggle even more. *Gravity.* What a funny concept.

The next thirty minutes were a blur of shaking hands and Marley being taken in for questioning- it wasn't a *small* bag of weed Funko had given him. Was he dealing? Where did he live? He stayed in a cell overnight while the facts were checked and filed away. As he sat on the hard bed of the cell, I think Marley filed away our friendship, too. 99 morning-after messages, and 0 replies. We never made eye contact, for the remaining 3 weeks of school. In fact, we barely made any kind of contact again. Last I heard, Marley moved across the country, to some prestigious university with a motto scribbled in Latin above every doorway. We don't speak anymore- I can count on one hand the number of times we have spoken, though Funko insists I exaggerate.

Funko became my friend, in a bizarre switch of fates… and my roommate a few years later. He decided to do a second degree, and I decided to go into student accommodation.

I still think about Marley, and I wonder if he thinks about me at all; I wonder if he blames me for almost ruining his life. He always had a flair for the dramatic. Funko and I chuckle about it in the earlier hours of some Sundays, when we can't feel our feet and the sky is uncomfortably blue, slowly fading into black. Sometimes I think the stars are Marley's teeth, and sometimes I think the whole thing was just a bad dream. Funko barely remembers Marley.

Tonight, I'm smoking for you, Marl.

Not Mine, but Part of Me

By S. Collins

The day she was born, I cried

Because she was beautiful, Black, American.

Amazing Grace was sung so soft and so sweet

It wasn't heard above the roars of

BACK WHERE YOU CAME FROM

NOT IN MY BACK YARD

The day she was born, I held her

Hurting for her

She was crying, not knowing why

Hungry, unaccepted by her country

Though she'd only been here half an hour

Already the Facebook feed throws out:

Is she Mexican? Adopted?

Mixed babies are so sexotic

**Exotic, lol

And for a minute she isn't my best friend's baby

She's an object for them to analyse

Physically, negatively, religiously

I wonder how old she'll be

When she's crying for different reasons

Than other babies.

Plague

By Victoria Croft
There's a plague in my city
It seeps through the streets
Kills the innocent
Infects the good

People are standing with their hands up
In surrender
Scared to touch anything
Wallets, phone, keys

There are people lying still
Eyes glassing over
Panicking as the air slips away
"I can't breathe"

It finds a vessel
And creeps deep inside
Wrapping and squeezing around the heart
Turning its victim blue

The death toll is rising
It's on the news every day
The system is collapsing
And Thoughts and Prayers aren't helping

There's a plague in my city
It's killing people in the streets
There's a plague in my city
And it's called the police.

<u>"And there was hope"</u>

By Milicent Fambrough

A hopeful day

of clapping

Turning into

Days of sacrifice

And there was hope

A time to step away

from what is comforting

To face things so uncomfortable

And there was hope

The mob is angry

Mourning of a nation

Pained conversations

And there was hope -M 6/2020

End's Beginning

By Jess Goode

I want to end the silence.

Not alone, because we are stronger

than I - the eye of the perpetrators.

Why do we glorify them in bronze,

and copper, in silk and satin, with riches

which make us seem

poor?

We are diverse,

in language, and in talent.

But we must all agree that silence must end.

We must speak, share the stories of our country. Not the twisted

lies

but the hidden

truths

as we delve

deeper,

discover, expose,

end

And live a new beginning

Starlight

By Jess Goode

When authority prevents change,

I want you to know I stand by you,

with you,

searching for meaning,

exposing incomplete secrets.

Because we've been commercialised,

they put a price on us,

but until the stars appear it's a price

we have to fight to see,

no matter how many tears we swallow,

names we choke on,

scars that sear from the outline

that isn't our outline, what they want

us to be.

Like the stars, when they dance, though,

we are beautiful,

we are the rivers that carry

their boats, their words

to an unknown

territory.

But it's one

we know

well.

And we'll never

be afraid

to hide behind clouds,

to wait for the moonrise,

to say

their names.

<u>Thus</u>

By Jess Goode

It's not just about giving them voices -

not a voice -

voices,

but also about giving them lives.

Lives, plural,

opportunities to be listened to,

to be

seen,

to be heard,

to be.

Eye-opening

By Jess Goode

I feel confused, the words

stick,

uncomfortable, at the back of my throat

but I know I cannot be silent.

I know I don't know enough,

I don't understand,

but I

stand.

I stand,

and I read -

read about a penetrating blue eye.

Beautiful, apparently.

But it's not in looks that beauty is found.

It's in words,

the words of people coming together

uniting in one cause

To give us a voice,

and for that voice to be heard

for change to come

to be listened to

even when the words don't quite come.

Lonely Earth

By Brian Judge

I KEEP FINDING THESE THINGS IN THE STREETS
I STILL HAVEN'T FIGURED OUT THEIR PURPOSE
THE ENDS ARE ALL BLOWN OFF... MAYBE THEY STORED MEDICINE?
NO MORE CRIES
I SHOULD MAKE A NECKLACE

THE CITY IS TOO IRRADIATED, I HAVE TO MOVE ON
THERE'S NOT MUCH ELSE OUT HERE THOUGH
BUT I CAN'T GET DISCOURAGED... TOO MUCH IS AT STAKE
I HAVE A GOOD FEELING ABOUT TOMORROW

I'M HAVING TROUBLE FALLING ASLEEP
MY MIND STARTS TO WANDER... WHAT IF I DIE OUT HERE?
NO ONE COULD HELP ME... NOBODY WOULD EVEN NOTICE
WHAT A LONELY WAY TO GO... DYING BREATHES LEFT UNHEARD

ITS TIME TO MOVE ON.
THERE'S A FOREST AHEAD. POSSIBLE LIFE.
I CAN'T SAY I'M NOT SCARED FOR WHAT AWAITS ME...
...BUT I CANT STOP. THIS IS BIGGER THAN ME.

I'VE STARTED MY JOURNEY TO THE FOREST TODAY.
WAIT...IN THE DISTANCE, IS THAT A HUMAN?
IS IT HOSTILE? MAYBE THIS IS A TRAP!
I HOPE I DON'T REGRET THIS
OVER HERE!!

HEY! HELLO!
HELLO?
CAN YOU HEAR ME?
WHEN I SAW WHAT IT REALLY WAS, I JUST FROZE...
NO
WE COULDN'T HAVE GOTTEN THIS BAD.
I DON'T KNOW IF I CAN GO ANY FURTHER...
WHATS THE POINT IF WE CAN ALSO BE SO UGLY?
MAYBE MANKIND FLED FOR A REASON...
MAYBE EVERYTHING DIED FOR A REASON...
I GUESS I'LL GO BACK HOME AND SHARE MY RESULTS.
HUH? THAT... THAT LOOKS LIKE...
?
LIFE!
THIS IS BIGGER THAN ME.

Revolt, Dismantle and Rise

By Kish Sofia

Do not pacify my pain

With your Spiritual bypassing

First, listen to my rage!

Because I no longer have the words

The Generational abuse towards my race

Makes me act out your violence

You systemically subjected me to

For over four hundred years and more

My colour will no longer

Be silenced

With your shame tactics

I have grown deep within my soul

My body has memories of my Ancestors

The trauma you have caused me

Through your manipulation

The legacy of your "White Supremacy"

To prevail at any cost to me or our Mother Earth

My voice is not divisive

There has never been any unity

In the first place

You only shushed me

And tried to bury me alive

Erase our stories for the humankind

Ah! The continued Genocide

That you cleverly hide

Surprise!

I am not dead

I am rising

Watch me

Don't forget brothers and sisters

I am but your mirror

Of your unconscionable ways

You built your corrupt system to serve you

With no conscience of the cruelty

You put me through

Beat me to the ground in my own land

You stole from me

So today

Have some respect

Pause for a minute

Understand the Colonial history and my pain

And do not shush me ever again

Behind the Poem:

This poem is a dedication to my brothers and sisters protesting out there on the frontline for the Black Lives Matter Movement. Your pain is my pain. I feel you. I hear you.

So much of this journey of evolution as a lifelong ally-ship with the Black and Indigenous community surfaced my own wounds from experiencing RACISM firsthand. There is no denying that it exists. In all the nooks and crannies we don't even realize even exist.

As a person of colour with both Brown and Indigenous roots, I too am part of the BIPOC (Black, Indigenous, People of Colour) group. But I am not here to debate and compare my individual pain with a movement that has been long standing for its overdue soul-debt owed to our Black and Indigenous Communities. I respect their movement and I have a deep love for their existence, culture and contribution to not only the American tapestry for our human story, but as part of our World Heritage.

Today is not the day to detail all the gruesome abuse, ill treatment, and hateful behavior of a few people that has shaped my heart's wounds forever. Racism is an ugly disease. And it is taught and passed on.

But, I just wanted to tell you that I know what it feels like to be the outsider in a place that is supposed to be your home. I know the ache an innocent heart feels when the one place in the world that seems to hold everyone else unconditionally… doesn't exist for you. I know what it feels like to wake up in terror and nightmares daily, wondering if you are safe. A profoundly felt rejection from the only place you've known since the day you were born when it will not hold you with pride. The only sentiment expressed is of judgement and degradation.

There are daily reminders, through subtle and blatant language, to force upon you the idea that your existence is unworthy. The thought of ever asking for more should never be an option. That was the expression of my encounter with "love" that was impressed upon me very early in my life. And I was born with privilege. However, with some miracle of life working its magic, I found my way to my own hero inside. But no one needs to suffer racism this way, in silence, while the system continues to build momentum in erasing rich history from our Human Experience. It is a tremendous loss to our collective soul as a Human Race to witness this erasure but more importantly to continue to allow it under our watch.

Now add that burden of pain I described earlier to a Black child who doesn't live in a safe neighbourhood, whose family has suffered generational trauma at the hands of a system that will never have their back. A Country their forefather's blood, sweat and tears built, (though that holds no value in the eyes of the world). They are told from birth that their existence is unwanted and that is all there is for their destiny. There is no romantic dream to aspire to. Patriotism is just a fantasy that avails only the white skin. This is more than four hundred years of bearing this pain of rejection daily. On top of that, they may also be a target to be placed in jail or brutally beaten to death for just existing and doing normal things.

What I am expressing to you, in essence, are the footprints left in the heart of a human by "Abandonment". Only an orphan would also know this feeling. And I attest to you that this type of rejection is choosing VIOLENCE against the oppressed, the under-privileged and the marginalized in our communities.

I urge you today to never again abandon them. We have to take the bold steps to heal our collective soul by acknowledging this pain first. True love is unconditional. And our heart is capable of true love in its essence. Finding ways to create action within our communities to start dismantling systemic racism is choosing true love for the Oppressed. Stone by stone, we will transform hate to love. I believe together we can. It's a beautiful, long road ahead of true courage and resilience.

Racism in the UK

By D. Relm

Where do I even start when it comes to Racism in the UK? We've convinced ourselves the Age of the Empire is over, we're no longer colonialists or slave-owners, we did Civil Rights before the United States... so how can we be racist?

Well, that's a great question. Up until a few months ago, I'd have told you we aren't. I live in a multicultural, technicolour neighbourhood. I've never worked under a white person, but I have worked under many Asian people, and everything felt fair. In years of work, there was never a racially-charged moment between us.

So, when Health Secretary Matt Hancock denied the UK is a racist place, I thought I knew where I stood. When he added, 'but more can always be done' I thought, *Well, which is it? Are we not racist, or can we do something against racism that definitely does still exist here?*

Of course, when the system is intrinsically racist, the system doesn't go around announcing it. Racism in the UK is in some ways worse than across the Atlantic- because the majority of Britons aren't aware of it. Racism in the UK lives at home, walks on the street, and most insidiously, it lives in our political and legal systems. I could add a line here about how Matt Hancock must have been living under a whitewashed rock his entire career, but we'll save that for later.

The UK uses words like 'tolerant' to describe our attitudes to people like minorities and immigrants. 'Tolerating' is a polite word for 'we'd rather you didn't, but we're not going to openly stop you'. I tolerate my dog's farts; I *welcome* his cuddles. I *accept* and *adore* his big cute smushy face... but I *tolerate* his nasty habit of barking at all hours of the night when he sees a spider.

Tolerance is not an anti-racist stance. It's a neutral one- which is the exact opposite of what we need, when people of colour are disproportionately punished by the legal system and are suffering in disproportional droves during the COVID-19 Pandemic.

Systemic racism may not be so visible on the multicolour streets of London, but when you look at the statistics, it's visible as blood on bath tiles. Asian workers are paid around 20% less on average than white British people, even if they're in the same work with the same level of education. Black Brits are paid almost 10% less than their white counterparts. And those are the minorities who have jobs- the unemployment rate of BAME Brits is twice the rate of white Brits.

Does this mean all employers are inherently racist? Of course not... but the system doesn't even look at where the motivations of an employer lie when they hire ten Caucasians and only eight People of Colour. The outcome of such hiring decisions is still discriminatory, no matter the conscious intentions of the hiring manager.

What do the figures tell us? For employers, the system is rigged in their favour; they are getting away with discrimination because our system lets them. The political system isn't clamping down, the public is either unaware or doesn't care to stop supporting these businesses (who I can't name here for legal reasons but who I'm sure you can find with a quick internet search).

Hate crime rates in the UK are twice as high as they were a decade ago. Police are almost ten times more likely to stop and search People of Colour, and stop-and-search warrants are more frequently placed over majority BAME neighourhoods like mine. When I walk around town with my Pakistani friends, more often than not, we are stared at; giving each other side glances that say 'we'll talk about this later, when it's safe'.

The UK government is committed, however, to tolerance over anti-racism. Maybe that's why we were all paying compensation for the 'loss' of slavery up until 2015- a fact that was only revealed because an official government social media account put it out as a 'fun fact'. Yeah, it must be *really* fun to be a Black Brit and know your taxes have been used to pay already wealthy people for the unjust ownership and objectification of your ancestors. *Super* fun.

And what about the British public? Recent surveys show almost 20% of British people agree with the idea of 'biological racism'- that is, the idea that people of different races are biologically different in terms of intelligence, for example. Almost half of the public believe some races are born harder-working than others. Just 25% of white British people believe in systemic racism.

But, movements such as BLM also had a high turnout in the middle of the COVID-19 pandemic. People of all races came out, knocked down statues of slave owners, protested against police brutality, and generally did what they could for racial equality, given the circumstances.

There's one thing we can do to help ourselves here: learn about the UK's history of Racism. Now, the timeline I have here is in no way an exhaustive list (and because this article is already long enough, I've left out the Pre-WWII stuff even though it is relevant), but it's a start. The rest is on you.

A Brief History of The UK's Racism:

1948: The Windrush Scandal

In 1948 a large group of Commonwealth (mostly Black Jamaican) citizens were brought from the Caribbean to Britain, with the government's OK, to help rebuild the country and bolster the economy after WWII. They did.

Fast forward to modern day, and the descendents of the Windrush generation who were born in the UK are facing crackdowns from the conservative government. They are losing their jobs, being deported to countries they aren't even from, it's just a nightmare.

1968: Rivers of Blood

Conservative Minister Enoch Powell delivered a speech in April 1968. The speech was full of racist and anti-immigration rhetoric that claimed to just be 'saying what the average working man in the street is thinking'. Powell advocated for the (white) British business owner's right to racially discriminate against his workers and warned his constituents of the 'madness' that is allowing immigrants into this country to marry and work and, you know, lead normal lives.

Powell's speech had quite a positive reception, even though he was fired for his vitriol. He received 100,000 letters of backing and London workers marched in solidarity with his views.

A new Commonwealth Immigrants Act was also passed, condemned by the European Human Rights Commission as 'racist, inhuman, and degrading'.

1965- The First Race Relations Act

This was the first law against racism/discrimination the UK had ever seen.

1976: The Race Relations Act

This act solidified the laws against discrimination that we still have in place today, making it illegal to discriminate against someone because of their race if you are:

- Employing them
- Training them
- Renting to them
- Educating them
- Or providing any other goods, facilities, and services to them

1976- The Grunwick Dispute

South Asian refugees and migrants were forced to leave their lives (especially persecution in Idi Amin's Uganda) and move to the UK with very little in the way of the possessions and wealth they had had in their home countries. Where they had been well-educated, middle-class citizens, in the UK they were forced to take more manual work in factories.

Most of these factory workers were women, and they were horrifically mistreated by the factory workers, who took great pleasure in humiliating the women. They had to ask to go to the toilet, if they were called into the office it was a form of public intimidation in front of the other workers, and they were seen as unskilled by wider society.

In August 1976, Jayaben Desai and a larger group of mainly women of colour walked out in protest against the way workers were treated in factories like Grunswick. The protest grew, and eventually turned into marches involving over 20,000 people. While the strikes ultimately failed, they still managed to improve conditions at Brunswick and go to show that nothing is more powerful than a group of women with a common mission.

1981- The Brixton Riots

Racial tensions escalated as young Black people protested police brutality that was constantly perpetrated against them. Over 5,000 people were involved in Brixton alone in an event that was dubbed 'Bloody Sunday' by newspapers. There were three days of rioting in London, followed by further protests throughout the UK, notably in Bristol and Leeds.

A public inquiry came to the conclusion that 'we just have a few rotten apples in the police, that's all' and did little to change the system that allowed those bad apples into their uniforms in the first place. However, new practices were put into place, the Police Complaints Authority was set up to supervise complaints against law enforcement.

1993- The Murder of Stephen Lawrence

Again, racial tensions were exacerbated by the actions of the police when Stephen Lawrence (aged 18) was killed in a racially motivated attack perpetrated by 4-6 young white men with prior records of racially motivated violence. The police took their sweet time arresting the culprits with the excuse that they did not know about arrest under 'reasonable suspicion' - a basic facet of criminal law that they *definitely* actually knew about. Only two of the culprits were convicted and even then only in 2012, with the police officially closing the case in August 2020.

The brutal murder of Stephen Lawrence led to an inquiry that concluded (in 1999) that the police were 'institutionally racist', and that their incompetence was not due to 'just a few bad apples'. A long time to wait for a small victory, but a necessary step in the greater fight to get the concept of institutional racism widely accepted.

2000- Race Relations laws were updated.

Now, all public authorities are responsible for fighting racism.

2007- The Racial and Religious Hatred Act

This made it a criminal action to threaten (either with words or behaviour) with the intent of stirring hatred against any race/group of people due to their religion or lack thereof.

As I said before, this list isn't exhaustive, and a quick search on the internet will tell you that. We have horrifically racist organisations such as Britain First and the

National Front. There have been a great deal of murders by police and ignored by police that we have yet to see explored in the news.

But Black people have been in the UK since 100 AD. There's a lot of history to catch up on; this article is just the jumping-off point. It's okay not to know right now- it's not okay to still not know in a week from now, when you've had time to digest everything we've said here.

Actions you can take in the UK:

- Write to your MP and Demand they condemn Trump's use of force against his own citizens, ask them to demand the government do more to tackle the BAME COVID-19 death rate in the UK.
- Support Black-owned brands.
- Join the campaign for curriculum reform: support the Black Curriculum's campaign for Black lived experiences throughout history and British colonialism to be taught in schools. Apply pressure by getting in touch with Secretary State for Education, Gavin Williamson, and your local MP.
- If you can't donate, fundraise, sign petitions, educate yourself on anti-racism and vote for MPs who actively stand against racism and prejudice.

Starting a Conversation with Your Racist Relatives

By D. Relm

As a teen, everyone around me was obsessed with politics. My friends had engaging Socratic debates every lunchtime about if Labour or the Conservatives were doing things right. My dad founded a viral online group for political discourse, and I... hated every minute of it all.

At dinner parties I'd tune out the second any election was brought up, knowing one side of the family was too conservative to cave and admit gay people should be able to marry and Black people are still oppressed; and the other side would be too liberal to admit political correctness and cancel culture can go too far sometimes. Minds are rarely changed when these conversations happen. Why participate when nothing ever changes for the better?

Lately, however, there's one subject I just can't stay quiet about: Racism. I figure if I'm going to die on any political hill, this one is the most deserving... if only because so many of my 'All Lives Matter' family members are willing to die on this hill too.

It's easy to stay quiet when you know nobody else at the table is going to agree with you. That's how this stuff has been going unchecked for so long. It's hard to talk about it, especially when you don't have any firsthand experience of oppression. But when there are so many people who do, it becomes imperative to educate yourself, educate your relatives, and anyone else within earshot. If everybody did that, there'd be a damn sight fewer people claiming 'Black people are the least oppressed nowadays'.

So, how do we have these tough talks? Here are some tips and mind tricks I and my friends have learned through experience.

Choose who you want to talk to. Maybe don't dive off the deep end with great-grandma Gladys who keeps those 'adorable' Blackface dolls in her china cabinet. Starting off with a person you know and trust and who may agree with you on some points but not others will help you grow in experience and confidence when it comes to having these hard conversations.

Keep things a Dialogue, not a Debate. In a debate, there's an ugly attitude of competition. Human rights issues (such as racism) are not a competition. In a dialogue, you are making an effort to learn attitudes and opinions from both sides, in an educational way. In a dialogue, you have to:

Show you're listening. Don't just nod along- repeat their words back to them, directly engage with their points, admit when they make a good point and acknowledge when they agree with what you say. Listen to *understand*, not to respond. When people feel heard, they're more likely to hear you back. Also, it's genuinely hard to interrupt someone who's repeating something you've said or is saying you have a good point, even if their argument is ultimately against yours.

Use their words to counter their arguments. When someone says they see why the protests are happening but don't agree with the riots destroying property, you can agree that the violence is needless. You can agree that it's good the protests are happening, because they're calling attention to an important issue. Then you can move onto the deeper stuff: *why* is the destruction of property happening? Why haven't the *peaceful* protests worked? Which brings me to my next point:

Do your research. Don't bluff your way through and make up statistics on the spot, not when everybody has the internet in their pocket and can instantly refute you with the touch of a button. If you talk about a study, make sure you know when it was and who conducted it. With so many people saying 'fake news' every time a fact doesn't match up to their opinion, it's vital you know your facts and are irrefutable. We all have that relative who seems to think the protests and riots are just an American response to George Floyd's murder, and not to hundreds of years of George Floyds internationally, institutional injustice, internalised racism, and inherently violent police training systems (particularly in the United States). When you know your facts, it's a lot easier to silence ignorance where you find it.

Experts say when a family member says something racist, the best thing to do isn't to jump in headfirst with a 'YOU'RE WRONG ABOUT THAT'. Instead, take some time to research, meditate, get your emotions of anger, anxiety and disbelief at who you share DNA with under control. Then come back to the person and begin the dialogue with a calm head.

Know the history of your race and your country, even if it isn't pretty. Even if it makes the bile rise in the back of your throat at the thought of your ancestors actively owning people. It's important to contextualise the time in which much of the current system was formed. Learn what privilege you have and who had to suffer so you could have it. You can also acknowledge your own internalised racism by undertaking an implicit bias test (easy enough to find online). This might give you a better mental platform to relate to your loved ones.

Stockpile your information. I have a word document that is full of links to articles refuting racist claims such as 'there is no wealth gap' and 'racism is a thing of the past'. Some of my relatives aren't the biggest readers, so when I come across any infographics or illustrated facts I save those so they can be sent to the people who need to see them. This may sound like pandering, and I'm not saying those non-readers shouldn't be doing their homework themselves, but in the early stages of de-brainwashing a bigot it's helpful to pander to them.

Show how you directly influence the Black experience. Knowing about microagressions, where our tax dollars are really going, all that jazz- that helps to show that not only is racism still going strong, but we are actively contributing to it, even if you claim you 'don't see colour'.

Don't let them make you angry. I get it- it's hard having these conversations. People are literally dying because we have been stalling talking about racism (internal and institutional) for so long. But when you get angry, that not only clouds your mind and leads you away from talking about solid facts, but it also makes you more likely to interrupt. It might be satisfying to tell great-aunt Karen that she doesn't know shit about the Black experience just because she watched *The Blind Side*, but hold your horses and remember point 1: show you're listening. If you're interrupting, you ain't listening. If you're calling them or their views bigoted, why are they going to listen to you?

If you do get angry and say something, apologise. Even if you don't want to, be the bigger person. Do you think you can change someone you don't talk to anymore because you called them a racist dickface? Nah. However accurate, clever, or flesh-searing your insults are, don't let them be the focus here.

Frame things from a personal perspective. This isn't the same as getting emotionally personal. This is prefixing what you say with things like 'to me' or 'the way I see it' or 'in my opinion, the lives of Black people matter more than stolen goods from any of the multibillion dollar companies who are doing the **opposite** of struggling in the current climate.' Using statements starting with 'I', such as 'I feel', 'I felt', or 'I've found' makes people less likely to mock what you're saying, because when you frame them this way then a mocking response looks like them mocking you... which makes them look like a dick.

Don't let them end the conversation by being non-racist. The ultimate goal of your discourse is to have them be anti-racist, because that's what the world needs right now. We don't need 'colour blind' people who 'see everybody as equals, because all lives matter equally.' This is why knowing your facts is important: institutionally, statistically speaking, the legal system values non-white lives less. A non-racist can still claim that killer cops are just 'bad apples'; an anti-racist cannot, because an anti-racist knows the problem is deeper than the occasional psychopath with a uniform. It helps here to admit that you do see colour, that colour doesn't need to be ignored because ignoring something only fuels the stigma against it. And yes, of course all lives matter, but until the system protects Black

lives, we need to keep screaming out: BLACK LIVES
MATTER.

To be clear, I'm not saying you have to 100%
change their minds or confront hundreds of years of racism
in one day. But give them something to think about when
the conversation is over that will leave their opinions at
least a little off-kilter, if they're honest with themselves.

**Keep the conversation focused on their views, for the
most part.** Ask active questions about their opinions. Be
openly, genuinely curious about why they think the way
they do. That way when you introduce your opinions, your
curiosity is more likely to be reciprocated.

Boundaries are healthy and necessary. Setting basic
expectations for a conversation before you have it is a good
idea- it can keep your expectations realistic, and when
someone crosses the line you can say things like 'I'd really
rather you not use that word' or 'I don't want to debate
about whether or not Black lives matter, I want to talk
about why you shared that pro-policing post.' If a relative
continues casually using racist slurs, or if they continue
using incendiary language like they're just trying to hurt
you or get under your skin, hell yeah you need to distance
yourself from that person. Preferably with an airplane, dyed
hair, and a fake passport. Psychologists even recommend
telling the offending loved one to expect to see less of you
in the future if they continue playing hopscotch on your
boundaries.

**Recognise it's not going to be easy, and prepare to get
very uncomfortable.** There will be disagreements,
arguments against you that can sound convincing
depending on how they're presented. You're absolutely

going to mess up, because nobody is perfect. The thing that matters is you're trying, you're educating yourself so you know what you're talking about, and you're talking.

Realise you can't change every mind, all you can do is try (and phone your politicians like mad to incite institutional change). Sometimes you need to stop a conversation, end of... well, end of conversation. Some people aren't going to change no matter what the facts are, no matter how many real experiences you throw at them. If a person is toxic, they're toxic. If you think it's right to change tactics and return to the topic at another time, do that. But don't waste your life in circular conversations.

Remember Racism wasn't built in a day. It won't be dismantled in a day either. It all starts with a conversation- and it will take more than a single conversation to make real change. Maybe you tackle a smaller topic, like the 'riots', or the broken policing system. Just don't try to infodump the last 400-ish years onto your conversation partner. The information won't sink in and you'll probably just come off as arrogant. Education takes a while, and on this path you don't just have to learn; you have to unlearn and re-learn.

Don't think that you can't talk about racism because you're white. I know some will find this one controversial, but white silence has perpetuated white violence for far too long. If we can't talk about things for fear of making mistakes or fear of cancel culture, nothing's ever going to change. Besides, how many white people do you know with an **equal** amount of white and POC friends? White people need to be educating white people. That's how ideas get mobilised, especially in more isolated communities where fewer POCs are given the opportunity to live.

Absolutely, promote Black and Brown voices. Don't think you know what it's like to be systematically oppressed, but you can learn from those who do and spread the information to other people who don't know.

Know when it's time to support the movement differently. If you're not the best talker, if your relatives are toxically stuck and don't respond to any reasonable attempts at dialogue, there are other ways to combat racism. Support Black-owned businesses and creators, donate to charities, volunteer, spread information online. Every little bit helps. It doesn't even have to be about racism- following Black models, artists, scientists, etc, diversifies your feed and gives a boost to people who need it.

How to Confront Racism Within Yourself

By D. Relm

An uncomfortable truth: I am racist. How about another: so are you. I hope neither of us are violent bigots who wear pillowcases and throw moltovs into peaceful protestors; but big acts of violence and discrimination aren't the only ways to be racist. It's an awful thought as a white person watching videos of police brutality: you might have more in common with the officer than the victim. Nobody wants to admit they have something in common with the killer, but we all do: unconscious bias. Becoming aware of our unconscious bias is important in helping us understand how to be less racist and how to help minorities in a world that feels built upon racist institutions and traditions.

Civil Rights movements made it not only immoral to discriminate against a person based on race, but also illegal. Now... weed is illegal in a lot of places, and we didn't stop smoking it just because we might get jail time or a fine. We just got more subtle about it, kept it in the home, made it a taboo topic.

'Aversive racism' is the term for when feelings of racial hatred are replaced with avoidant behaviours and uncomfortable feelings, often without you actually noticing, because you don't label yourself a racist- you're a good person! It's when the white woman sees the Black man walking towards her and crosses the street. It's when the only Black girl in your class isn't sure when to sit, and nobody's looking at her, so she sits alone. Where only a small percentage of people are vocal, violent, old-fashioned style racists, a significant amount of people are aversive racists due to their implicit biases, their unconscious beliefs.

Nobody with a rational mind *wants* to be a racist. That's good, but it's also a barrier when it comes to recognising your own biased ideas and behaviour. Example: you interview two candidates for a job interview. One is white, one is Black. They both show up in suits, they both have the same degree from the same university and the same number of years in the same type of work experience. How do you decide who to hire? Well, the white person looked more professional, right? The Black guy let his hair grow out in what could easily become an afro one day. Let's go with the white guy, just in case.

RED FLAG!

RED FLAG!

RED FLAG!

Often when these cases do occur in real life, the interviewer will unconsciously change the criteria to benefit the white person. It's not always obvious as haircut discrimination. When this goes unchecked, it perpetuates everything that interviewer might consciously be against: class divides, the wealth gap, and the disproportionately high unemployment rate of POCs. When we don't monitor ourselves, we don't monitor when we're behaving in a discriminatory way. Simple. It's an unconscious bias because *you aren't conscious of it.*

So, what can you do?

Well, **talk to People of Colour**. It's called 'aversive racism' because we often unconsciously avoid POCs.

When we talk as people, even if we look different, that reinforces in our minds 'this person is just like me.' The more you talk to people outside your ethnic/racial group, the more you learn about how they see the world, the struggles they face, their culture, what shows they like to watch. The more you teach your unconscious that 'people are people, not threats.' Talking to people doesn't erase every unconscious demon in your brain, but it's a baby step.

Sometimes, **it's our fear of being perceived as racist that makes us actually act racist**. If you don't talk about race, if you don't have any non-white friends, you're not being challenged. You're 'safe'. You're not at risk of saying anything racially insensitive. The more open you are to making mistakes and being corrected without labelling yourself a racist forever, the less likely you are to be an actual racist. You can't make an omelet without breaking a few delicate white eggs, right?

Remember **you are not your unconscious biases**. You're also not your conscious moral values. You're a mixture of both, and that's reflected in your actions.

Don't ignore differences. When you say you're 'colourblind', that means you don't see the struggle, oppression, and everything else Black people and other POCs go through on a daily basis. You don't see the beauty of their different cultures and different physical appearances. Isn't it better to live in a complicated technicolour world than a bland grey one?

Think about how you're the same as people who look different from you. Yes, you see their colour, but you both love grilled cheese. You both love crappy superhero films and both of you have really weird conservative relatives who would DIE if they knew you had a friend outside your 'normal' group, whatever that means. Everyone has something in common with the person sitting next to them, it's just a matter of finding out what it is.

When you do notice the implicit bias of yourself and others, call it out. Say, 'this is not acceptable, that's not the standard I want to live up to.' Then you set actual standards for yourself, and you hopefully help people who are being discriminated against, too.

Look at the bigger picture. When you understand the racism within yourself, look for it in the system. How does police training play with the unconscious mind of the officer? How does the system, while wearing a disguise of equality, keep Black people and POCs making lower incomes, in 'worse' neighborhoods, at higher risks for just about everything? What about at the most important formative levels of humanity- school? Studies have been conducted where teachers were more likely to see a Black child's face as angry than a white child's, even if the kids had the same facial expression. How can we *begin* to fix that?

I know it's hard work. I *know* you're not racist. But you also are, and if you don't take some stock about that, then you'll stay part of the problem. Luckily, you can be part of the solution; but it all starts with you. What standard will you hold yourself up to?

How to Talk to Your Kids About Racism

By D. Relm

I know what you're thinking: *I don't have to teach my kids that much about racism. They're too young for it. They'll learn when they're older.*

And that's great if you're white, but for minority kids there is no such thing as 'too young'. They grow up in a biased world, and when the world is biased against you in particular, you notice; no matter how young you are.

Kids learn about race from their parents first- parents are like blueprints for kids as they grow. How does mommy treat daddy? Okay, that's how I want to be treated. What politics is good and what's bad? Okay, I'll vote for X Party. We might think kids can't pick up on the nuances of life, but that's so very, very wrong.

As early as six months old, a baby can notice racially-based differences in faces. Between the ages of two and four, they internalise racial bias. By 12, they are mostly set in their beliefs. Sure, you can change when you're an adult, but it's a hell of a lot harder than changing when you're a kid. So, parents, guardians, and cool aunties, you have just over a decade to make sure your kid doesn't become a racist asshole.

Don't think you can just avoid the subject, either. We live in a world entrenched in racial politics. Your kid is gonna pick up something in school. Even if they sleep through every class, they'll be awake on the playground and notice there's nuance to the social hierarchy. If you're silent, you're reinforcing the subconscious idea that race (and therefore racism) isn't a topic to be talked about, which might reinforce aversive racism for your child later in life.

So, what can you do for your children?

Talk to them. Don't pretend the problems in the world aren't real. Encourage your children to learn about other cultures, make friends with people from diverse backgrounds, etc. Learn *with* them, don't just lecture them. This is a bonding opportunity for you and your child as much as it is a learning curve.

Be the model for them to follow. This doesn't mean you can't make mistakes in front of the kid- in fact, please do! Own your mistakes, make sure your children see you dealing with your own internal biases. We live in a society where mistakes too often are the gateway to giving up rather than learning, growing, and succeeding. What you do every day matters, whether it's supporting Black businesses or taking your kids to that Asian food fair where you're one of very few white faces in the crowd.

Make your own multicultural connections. As stated above, you are the model for your kids to follow. If you are accepting of other cultures, your kids will be too. Not everyone can afford to travel to different countries (though if you can, it's certainly a world-broadening experience), but everyone can strike up a conversation with someone different to them. A big excuse people make to not talk about racism is lack of personal experience- well, give yourself some experiences!

That's not to say you should be friends with someone just because they're Black or Asian. You can be multicultural in other ways- exploring cuisines, books, and films from other cultures are great ways to get involved without looking for a 'token' friend.

Know your own privilege and prejudices, as well as those in your community. Growing up in a Catholic family and being friends with the only Muslim family for miles, I got a crash course in dealing with community prejudices and how to deal with friends who don't accept each other on principle. It wasn't until adulthood that I stepped back and examined the internalised prejudice, how growing up in a racially charged environment shaped me. When I did the work on myself and acknowledged the privilege and prejudice within, I was better equipped to talk to others about race and cultural differences- even my little nieces and nephews.

Now, those are all well and good tips, but how do you actually go through with the conversation about racism? It's hard enough talking to adults about it, nevermind mini-adults.

Younger kids have no filter and WILL point out differences like skin tone or visible cultural things like headscarves. Rather than shy away from the differences, you might make a remark like 'Isn't she pretty?' or 'That's a lovely scarf'. Statements that normalise differences will also remove taboos that your children aren't even aware of.

Be open when your child asks a question. Kids don't know what political correctness is, so when they mess up don't treat it like a big deal- calmly correct them and make sure they know it's okay to come to you with questions and thoughts about the world. If you have a big negative reaction or quiet them immediately with no explanation, it just reinforces the taboos you're trying to eliminate.

Be involved with their school. Attend events for parents and actively ask how the school is tackling racism, or how they are teaching the history of racial discrimination- and if they aren't, hold them accountable; ask why not.

When they get older, of course kids will be more aware. Some schools might even touch on Civil Rights in their curriculum, but no minimum-wage-paid teacher is having the deep conversations that need to be had with a bunch of pre-teens. So, it's your job as a parent to do things at home. Have open talks about race, diversity, and prejudice. Talk about stereotyping, the media, the justice system, etc. Keep the kids involved by relating it back to their favourite things, like the representation in Star Wars, for example- a franchise that started in the 80s and has continued and expanded to include multiple races and more female representation in modern times. What do they think of that?

Asking questions and just being an engaged parent is the bare minimum, but it's worth repeating: knowing how things are going at school and on social media keeps you and your kid engaged with the immediate community, and any instances of prejudice there. Be interested in what they're reading in their media and show they can come to you for advice when things get uncomfortable or confusing for them.

Family movie nights can also be a good tool for conversations. Movies like *Selma* or shows like *Dear White People* are catalysts for you to ask your (older) child, 'how did you feel about this?' or 'has anything like that happened at school?' Again, keeping the conversation open and providing a safe, nonjudgmental space for your child to express their opinions is the key to understanding how they see race and prejudice, how it effects them (or doesn't) in their daily lives.

When kids are over twelve years old, their adult opinions are pretty much already formed. So pay attention: what do they know? What have they experienced in their lives up till this point, regarding diversity and discrimination? Try your best to understand their thoughts and experiences, and keep the conversation going for a lifetime. The older your kids get, the more fun the conversations: you can add in complexities like different opinions and current headlines, etc. You'll be surprised how adult some kids are, when it comes down to it.

Encourage actions that are in line with their beliefs. Most kids are social media activists before they even know what they're fighting about. When the choice is conscious, safe, and when they're old enough, encourage them to attend protests and events. A young, educated, mobilised population is what the world needs if we're going to tackle over four hundred years of oppression and racist institutions.

Okay, but what do I actually say?

When your kid notices a racial difference, make sure they know there's nothing wrong with that, and also make sure they know it's not right to make judgements of people based on race or ethnicity.

Make being different a positive thing, not a negative thing. Don't create a sense of 'Other' or 'Us and Them'.

Talk about stereotypes; gradually take them apart and show how they are wrong: not all people of one group are the same.

Teach them history. Civil Rights, Jim Crow, Malcolm X, etc. You can talk about the history of certain stereotypes, appropriations, and racial slurs. History is important to help us and especially children understand things like microaggressions, why words hold power over marginalised groups and how some words should not be used, ever.

Show them how to actively be anti-racist. Am I saying take your toddler to a protest or riot? Hell no! But show them kindness, teach them to be kind and to listen to marginalised voices, to treat them with the same respect they would like to be treated with, etc. Talk about your own experiences, failures, and could-have-done-betters. Humanise the discussion, and you're halfway there already.

Remember it's okay not to know all the answers to all their questions. Parents put big expectations on themselves and it's easy to get overwhelmed when talking about big topics you might not have firsthand experience of. And that's **okay**- not knowing something is just an opportunity for you to learn and grow; and your children along with you.

It all starts with asking your children questions, letting them ask questions back, and having a dialogue rather than a lecture. Racism can't be cured in a day, and it can't be fully comprehended from one or two discussions either. So make conversations about deep issues a regular thing in your family, if they aren't already.

I Kneel,

By Liz Rivers

I will kneel, because I have family members who won't.

I will kneel, for the Black nurses taking care of my racist grandparents

I will kneel in the face of history itself, built not on my blood but on theirs

I will kneel for a movement that respects Black lives

I will kneel in apology for the my microagressions

I will kneel in solidarity, knowing I cannot understand

But I stand

I stand not for the family members

Who had the guts to share a post proclaiming

ALL LIVES MATTER

I stand not for the aunt who called them Letterboxes

I will not kneel for the grandfather who called George a thug

I will never again be one of them

I would rather be alone

Than accepted in a family

Who would not accept my child has a right to live

If she is the 'wrong' skin colour

Who would not love my husband as an equal

If his white smile stands out bright against dark skin

Who would call my child a macchiato and not a person.

Robin Hood and the Riot Shield

By Liz Rivers

Robin Hood stole from the rich

To give to the poor

When we protest against the police

They ask what for

He wore a mask to hide himself

But when we do the same

They pull it away with our health

Replace it with pain

Do they ever stop to wonder

Why Robin was the Hero

And the Sheriff was the villain?

Will they pause to *actually* protect,

To take in this moment

Let us breathe

Let *themselves* breathe

To ask themselves, really,

Are you the hero or the villain?

What Will You Do

By Liz Rivers

What will you do when you're holding the gun?

What will you do, when it's pointed at your son?

Will you admire what's in his brain,

Or splatter it on the pavement in pain?

What will you choose in the voting booth,

The ugly lies or the ugly truth?

When will you create something new?

Wishes

By Liz Rivers

How many men gotta play this game

Where they die and go to heaven in Government's name?

When are we gonna understand

We gotta be good to our fellow man?

In the internet we find every story ever told

We find everything but the truth

Which grows over our history like mold.

If you knew what his life was really worth

You'd have lifted your knee

Let him continue life on Earth.

I wish you saw the Black in your soul

And not on his skin

I wish you hadn't been on patrol.

Realisation

By Liz Rivers

I was older than I should have been when I realised I was white.

'All lives matter.'

'I don't see colour, that doesn't matter to me.'

'Live and let live! Why does everything have to be identity politics?'

It made sense that the teacher always got Laquan's name wrong, and never mine

Laquan is a weird name, we can't be expected to know everything

And of course there's nothing wrong going on when you cross the street

When someone with a melanin-mind stares at you

That's just staying safe, clinging to white crowds in white towns

As long as you watch a tv show or two with one character who doesn't look like you

You're not a racist, you're same as anybody else

White, Black, brown or blue

There's no difference between me and you.

I was taught we bleed the same blood, and that means
racism is dead

On the inside, we're all red.

I never knew I was white

Even as I opened the headlines and saw another Black man
shot dead

And sure, Black lives matter, but all lives do too

Just because an old relative is racist is no reason to cut ties

You just bite your tongue and listen, knowing the lies.

And I had brown friends, sure,

They showed me their fashion, culture, food;

And I loved to learn more

I asked them about racism and they got a look in their eyes

A lip-biting memory-fighting look in their eyes

As they said 'No, never'

And I breathed a sigh of relief.

I never knew I was white

Until He didn't come home to his daughter

She rang the doorbell and said she was sorry, but could she use my phone?

Only eight years old, not meant to be all alone

Her big brown eyes shining wide

Like her Father's never would again

Tears plump as Officer

She cried

Officer was up to no good

Especially when he saw

Her Father wearing a hood

And He was on video screaming, spectators livestreaming

Eyes wide like hers and everyone watching knew how it was going to end

That it *was* going to end when Officer kicked Him in the head

He was Black, in pain, getting kicked again and again

'I've had enough!'

But Officer didn't listen to that stuff

'Resisting arrest'

With a broken nose and blood in His eyes

An accidental death

But there was no accident, we all saw

Her father on the floor

And I knew if His blood was the same as mine

He'd have come home.

I wanted to scrape the white from my skin and give it to Him

But it was too late

So now I kneel in anger and shame and listen to His daughter's pain

And hope one day the great lies I told will come true

But all lives don't matter

Until Black lives do.

This is My World

By Qasim Shan

We all carry an identity when we are born; thrust upon us without any thought of what it would mean in an uncertain world. I've always been an ordinary person, yet nobody would ever see it that way. I was born to be prey, to be hunted by those guarding their families against bearded men speaking in sharp tongues with towels wrapped around their heads.

I was too young to remember the plane crash that changed the world. It was 2001 and I was only three at the time. Somehow, I do recall Mum sitting me down with tears welling in her eyes. My father was listening to the monotonous words of the tanned reporter coming through the small TV.

TERRORIST ATTACK ON US SOIL

THOUSANDS DEAD, A NATION STAGGERED AS TERRORISTS STRIKE

US PRESIDENT DECLARES WAR ON TERROR

Men, women, children were pulled from the rubble, but I didn't care. I just looked towards the small Superman

toy hanging from the fireplace and quickly ran away to play
with it.

As a child, I spent most of my time with Mum. She
dragged me along to wherever she would go, whether it
was the town centre or a quaint grocery store nearby. But
soon, I would notice something. She always kept her eyes
on the ground, and as we shuffled past people, they would
say something to her, but Mum's gaze remained
unwavering. I would soon learn why.

To those that passed by us, we were beacons of
death. Her mere existence provided humanity with an
excuse to attack us, and we would never forget it. I would
have to fight to survive; an undertaking that no child should
ever have to suffer through, but that didn't matter. The
nightmares arrived regardless, and its inception began in
September 2003.

I attended Beauden Primary School, with its complex
spanning for what seemed like miles, and the grim decor
crafted as though it were by the ancestors of an eccentric
billionaire who only came out at night. I would stare at the
building for a moment whenever Mum dropped me off, and
my visions of a dark man kneeling upon the cracked

gargoyle shattered quickly as the pasty-faced kids followed me inside.

"Oi, Paki, how long til' we go up in flames, eh?" I looked back; four glaring at me. Fuck. The classroom was stuffy so I sat at the front next to the slightly open window. There was a decent breeze there. The taunts continued as I waited for the teacher to begin the lesson. The same question was whispered behind me for a month until I finally answered. Seeing the blood rush from their faces made me smile. My parents weren't as happy about it though when called in.

"Not my fault," I muttered again and again as my mother glared at me throughout the meeting. She thanked the teacher, along with my father who had buried his head in his Samsung D-500, and they swiftly brought me home. To my surprise, there were no words thrown with anger.

All Mum would ever say was, "This world isn't ours but try to make it just a little smaller." That made no sense, so I ignored her and watched *Timothy Goes to School*. I had a jam sandwich as well.

I returned to school the next day and came home with a bloodied scalp. Verbal taunts now became much more physical, with their favourite pastime involving throwing me to the ground during football practice and claiming it as a solid tackle.

A new kid joined two years later, in Year 3, and he quickly wrestled them to the ground when Mr. Ashraf turned away to flirt with his assistant. The kid was called Ismael, and they left us alone because of him.

"Not many of us here, innit." Ismael huffed to me during the walk back to the changing room. He also mentioned how shit we both were at football.

"We're gonna have to stick together, *yarra*," I replied in our native tongue of Punjabi.

We progressed through primary school together and entered another realm in 2010; Sir Tom Thurnsby Community College. I gleefully looked at the masses and saw people who looked and spoke like me. Perhaps this route of education would be more my speed, I thought.

Not a damned chance.

STT was an interesting paradox; so many different ethnicities, cultures and religions... yet somehow segregated. The only Black guy walked alone, the white folk stayed in the Arts department, and the Pakistanis roamed everywhere looking for new ways to annoy the Bengalis. With my friends, I gained a newfound sense of confidence in a life I had previously carried with shame. During Year 7, we would try one-upping each other with antics of mild anarchy. We progressed from flicking pieces of rubber at students at the front of the class to throwing 300-page science books. I had almost taken someone's head clean off with the AQA resource, and when Dr. Sarwar returned to students quietly sobbing, she figured out pretty quickly that it was because of the small brown kid at the back struggling to stifle his laughter. That was the first time I ever received detention, and it wouldn't be the last.

We would continue making trouble throughout the year, with very few rallying against us.

"The fuck you lookin' at?" Ismael snarled at anyone who even hinted at having an issue. Their facades of bravery instantly shattered and they would hurry away with their tails limping between their legs.

"Look at 'em run." We laughed in the canteen queue. After eating our chicken tikka sandwiches, we dragged ourselves across the open playground to the astroturf. We scrambled to get on our torn Nike trainers, but the Sports Councilor, Mr. Davis, (a tall redhead) often closed the gate early.

"What the fuck, man?" I groaned, and he would scratch his scruffy chin, blaming us for eating first.

"You're a penchode, you know that, Phil?" Ismael loudly taunted, forcing us to run back the way we came. An hour later in Biology, a spectacled Asian teacher, who addressed himself as 'Lord Rashid', branded us with report cards and suspensions for when we would start Year 8. He also rang our parents when we refused to apologise for telling a teacher to fuck his sister. I wasn't allowed out of the house for a month.

Year 8 began the same; we were childish but no longer children. Detentions and reprimands were a daily regularity, but there was a new addition; a white guy who was in all my classes. He kept to himself, always scribbling incoherent symbols onto his exercise book. It was after Christmas when he joined the 'Afterschool Club', and Ismael found himself excluded for a week, so I was stuck, as each second achingly passed by, with someone who coughed like a chain-smoker on his deathbed.

"Drink your fucking water, man." I groaned at the echoes bouncing off the empty room.

"I didn't think of that, mate." He retorted with a sarcastic wave of his empty bottle. I smiled at the makeshift Superman logo he had drawn on the label. After we served our time, we walked different paths home.

Afterwards, I paid more attention to him. He was unusually calm among the ethnic population, and I was also surprised when we were paired together in Design Tech. The silence between us was deafening so I decided to alleviate the mood of the entire class with a rather spectacular rendition of *The Lion Sleeps Tonight,* By The Tokens. Year 8 was almost over, but his participation was the most shocking surprise.

"IN THE JUNGLE, THE MIGHTY JUNGLE, THE LION SLEEPS TONIGHT!" I screamed at the top of my lungs.

"A-WEEMA-WEH, A-WEEMA-WEH, A-WEEMA-WEH, A-WEEMA-WEH!" He continued the ballad and I was slightly taken aback by it.

We were tone deaf and hit all the wrong notes, but it was the first time I had almost collapsed from laughing. He patted me on the back as we left for lunch and introduced himself as Daniel. He told me to call him Danny.

Year 9 and 10 went by in a flash, and it was only at the beginning of Year 11 when I realised I had become someone else. The 'Brotherhood' had long since shunned me and their resentment was quite clear. As I would walk past them, Ismael would loudly boast about his Snapchat videos showing 'memorable' nights out with his ilk with myself nowhere nearby. I was glad because asking Mum for money to inhale mango-flavoured smoke was getting on her nerves. I never did once join in, to be honest, because finding a way to make a Buxton water bottle last four hours was far more entertaining.

It was about then when I began lying about being ill so that I could get out of visiting dingy lounge bars in Manchester. Instead, I accepted Danny's request to join him at his home. If I had known he invited others, I never would've come. I knocked on the door, and it swung open with the host welcoming me inside a home brimming with people for whom that I had made life hell. They stared at me as I followed Danny. I felt weak and unsure of myself. A pale girl I faintly recognised from my year sauntered up to me, with a drink in one hand and a sandwich in the other. She was the only one who introduced herself.

"Danny said you'd come. I'm Jess!" The short girl with a fringe smiled as she reached over to hug me. I wasn't comfortable at all, but that didn't stop her. I refused the drink she offered me, not out of spite, but because I didn't want to return home smelling of alcohol. I wanted to live a few more years.

As the weeks went by, I finally summoned the courage to talk to Jess more. I turned out to be a decent conversationalist when racial slurs weren't involved. Not to mention, she was the most beautiful person I had ever seen. Why she'd want to talk to me was quite confusing, and I was even more bewildered when she added me on Facebook and chatted more throughout the night.

We returned to school after the Easter half-term, and Jess couldn't wait to introduce me to her friends hiding away in the Music room.

"This is Qasim!" she spoke enthusiastically, as she pushed me forward. I smiled, as it was the only part of me that could move. A mass of theatre students then hugged me but for some reason, I felt anxious. Perhaps it was because I was the only brown guy to have ever voluntarily stepped foot in there, but the chorus of voices greeting me was worth it though.

"It's great to meet you, Qas."

Was it really? I felt ridiculous, as though I was a chained freak being looked up and down; with a large nose and thick sideburns from a pitiful attempt to grow a beard as just a few of my physical imperfections, I wasn't the best ambassador they could've had, but they seemed happy enough.

Exam season was now coming to an end, and I was considered to be a good friend of theirs. A slight sense of unease remained towards me, however. I hadn't talked to

Ismael since Year 11 began, but that didn't matter. Those I had once proudly associated myself with were still hounding my friends. I knew that I would end up having to pay for the history I tried to sweep under the rug, but I just wished it hadn't happened the way it did.

21st May 2014; the last ever day of high school. Danny and I were talking about the choices we faced ahead but also wondering where the hell Jess was. I looked at the canteen and saw Ismael leaving. He glared at me and forcefully barged into her. Jess tripped and fell, smashing her plate of pasta on the floor.

We rushed towards her and helped her up. Her knee was grazed and bloodied.

"Why don't you watch where the hell you're walking?" I yelled.

Ismael stopped and turned.

"You talkin' to me, you fuckin' *gora*?"

"Piss off," Danny interjected, moving swiftly in front of me. I tried to move forward too, but a crowd of students circled us, anticipating a spectacle.

"Repeat it, white boy. I fuckin' dare ya."

Danny's fingers curled tightly. Jess winced as I helped her limp towards the table behind us. I saw her eyes widen before instinctively flinching at the punch thrown my way. I stumbled back and loudly gasped for air. My jaw cracked slightly with every laboured breath, but I gritted my teeth and climbed back up, only to see Ismael punch Danny and then hurry towards me with his arms reaching to wrap themselves around my neck. Danny was standing with his fists raised, but his nose was bleeding profusely into his mouth. I couldn't breathe, but I could still find a way to piss Ismael off.

"You're a bit of a cunt." I managed to muster, seeing Danny smirk behind his fists and I groaned at Ismael's elbow slamming into my back. At that moment, I managed to break away, and Danny tackled him to the ground. Our scuffle lasted for 5 minutes before anyone else had the balls to step in. When they pulled us away, Ismael wiped the blood away from his mouth, and Danny was lying still on the floor. I broke my arm in four places too.

A month passed before Danny was able to talk to us again. On the odd day or two, I slept in the hospital overnight with

Jess joining me when he was finally able to sit upright. Danny swore as his stomach creased but he smiled in between the coughs he spat.

"You got some money for a drink?" I whispered with a grin. Jess laughed. Danny replied with a firm middle finger. I left them to catch up and pulled out two pounds. I groaned as my cast cracked a little. My arm hadn't fully healed yet. Shuffling patients left their rooms, followed by nurses with their patience running thin. I chuckled to myself as I pressed the buttons on the vending machine. I grabbed the fallen water bottle and walked back into a room filled with hearty laughter.

It's early 2018 now, and we're still closer than ever. Danny and I are English undergraduates meanwhile Jess is acing her Musical Theatre studies. We're standing together in a world that's a little smaller; but even though the nightmares won't end soon, if ever, I'll still be around to fight fear with hope.

This is my world. It always has been.

A History of Racism in the United States

By J.R.R. Stewart

What we call the Civil Rights movement took place in the US from 1955 to 1965, although its history is far broader and is arguably still being made today. The movement aimed to pressure the US government into giving equal rights to all Black American citizens.

At the end of the Civil War in 1865, slavery was made illegal in the US. This by no means ended racism or discrimination against Black Americans. Slavery itself is actually still legal- as punishment for a crime (hence why US citizens in jail can be made to work for literally no money). The prejudice and violence faced by Black Americans has continued on well into the 20th and 21st Century.

Jim Crow laws

During the Post-Civil War Reconstruction Period, Black people experienced freedoms that they never had before in the newly United States. They held positions in public office and sought changes to give them the right to vote.

In 1868, the 14th amendment gave Black Americans equal protections under the law. Later on in 1870 the 15th amendment gave them the right to vote. However, the people in the South (who were still sore from losing the Civil War and being forced to give up their human property) weren't very happy with having to share their Civil Rights with Black people, and so came the Jim Crow laws.

 The Jim Crow laws legally allowed segregation across the Southern states. In a nutshell:

- Segregation was enforced in bus/train station waiting rooms, at water fountains, in restrooms, building entrances, elevators, cemeteries, and even certain cashier windows.
- Black Americans could not live in white neighbourhoods, go to white schools, or use white pools, phone booths, hospitals, asylums, jails, or residential homes for the elderly and disabled.
- In certain states, prostitutes were segregated according to race.
- Interracial marriage and even co-habitation became illegal.
- Perhaps most disturbingly, in order to vote, a literacy test had to be undertaken first… Unless you could provide proof of adequate education (which the majority of Black people could not, being former slaves or descendants of former slaves).

You may be thinking that a literacy test wouldn't be too hard to pass. But you'd be wrong, questions in such tests were often confusing and irrelevant, such as 'How many bubbles are there in a bar of soap?' or incredibly obscure historical knowledge that they wouldn't know because of their lack of access to proper education.

Not only that, but of course the test was just as segregated as the rest of society at the time. Where a white applicant who couldn't prove their education to a sufficient standard would also have to sit the test, the questions and tasks they were given were often far easier. A white applicant may be asked to read or copy a sentence from the constitution to prove their literacy. A Black applicant, on the other hand, might have to copy a whole paragraph of the constitution not from a text but from a dictation- dictation meant a mumbling white examiner and therefore another easy way to suppress the Black vote.

Jim Crow laws made it near impossible for Black citizens to run for office in order to actually change things. Any who did were guaranteed to be getting a visit from the KKK, and a lovely gift of a burning cross in their front garden, just in case they didn't have enough to worry about already.

The Northern states didn't adopt the Jim Crow laws, however Black Americans there still experienced discrimination at their jobs, whenever they tried to buy a house or go to school... or, you know, generally coexist.

To make matters worse, Southern segregation gained ground in 1896 when the Supreme Court declared in the Plessy vs Ferguson case that facilities for Black and white people could be 'separate but equal'. Basically, now there was a 'legal distinction' between how Black and white people could be treated; and you'll never guess who came out on top...

Housing Laws and Redlining

During the 'new deal' (Franklin D. Roosevelt's fix for the wall street crash), housing issues were made a top priority.

FDR believed that American home ownership was essential for economic survival. Two new agencies were created, the first was the Home Owner's Loan Corporation (HOLC), the second was the Federal Housing Administration (FHA). HOLC was created to give home loans to Americans that weren't as financially taxing as a mortgage, something that would bankrupt most due to the huge interest rates at the time. The FHA focused on standardising quality construction and insuring loans for home building.

This all sounds great: Americans could get better access to housing as well as loans that they could easily pay off, ensuring they could keep their house and have no risk of homelessness. How great!

...Until you hear about redlining, a practice designed by pro-segregation politicians that made it almost impossible for Black Americans to get a home loan that would cover the cost of a house. Most could barely make rent with their loans.

Redlining worked by splitting neighbourhoods into red areas and green areas. If you lived in a green area you were able to get a better home loan and would be more likely to be able to buy a house in another green area. Living in a red area meant you got a lower home loan; most of these loans wouldn't even cover the cost of a house inside another red area, let alone a green one.

Red and green areas were decided on economic factors. Poorer areas were designated as red areas and more affluent areas were green. The new deal had introduced many new job opportunities and had allowed Americans to recover financially from the effects of the Great

Depression. Most of the high paying jobs were almost exclusively held by white citizens, meaning that green areas were almost entirely white and red areas were almost entirely Black.

As a result of this practice, the wealth gap between races increased even more than before and eventually resulted in what we know today as suburbs and gated communities. One of few Black families that could afford a house in the suburbs in the South were quickly pushed out by the constant violence and racist abuse directed towards them. When they moved in, there were protests attended by people that didn't even live in that neighbourhood, saying that the suburbs were for whites only. The Black family were quickly pushed back into a red area, despite their economic status.

Believe it or not, this practice still exists today in the US. On top of this, funding for schools is also decided on economic factors, with richer areas receiving more funding for education. As a result, Black Americans are less likely to receive a high quality of education; less likely to go to college and get a high earning job that would allow them to move to a green area. This is more or less a completely legal form of segregation. For further information, look into the 'wealth gap' that currently exists in America. While white people were allowed to acrue ancestral wealth for the 400+ years of slavery, Black people were not and were therefore already at an economic disadvantage, even before redlining.

World War II

 Before the beginning of World War II, most Black
Americans worked as low paid farm hands, servants, or
factory workers. Past 1940, there was a lot of war-related
work available. The US didn't join the war until December
of 1941, meaning that they were able to re-industrialise at a
massive pace providing weaponry to the Allies.

 Most Black Americans weren't given the better
paying jobs, swapping one form of factory work for
another. Even when the US did join the war, they were
actively discouraged from joining the army.

 This changed in June of 1941 after Roosevelt
signed an executive order making all war-related jobs
available to citizens regardless of race, religion or gender.
He only did this after thousands of Black Americans
threatened to march on Washington in protest, which could
have ended the progress the government was making in re-
industrialising.

 Although finally allowed to join the military, Black
citizens still experienced the same segregation they did
back home; with many platoons being made Black-only.
The Tuskeegee Airmen is the most famous of these. They
were the first Black military aviators in the US army air
corps and gained 150 distinguished flying crosses. They
were considered among the best pilots the US military had
at its disposal.

 Despite the great service Black Americans had done
for their country, and the fact that the US claimed they had

initially entered the war to 'defend freedom and democracy', the same everyday racism was still there when Black soldiers came back home.

Towards the beginning of the Cold War, president Truman signed an executive order to end discrimination in the military. This was done after protests by Black veterans. These events set the stage for the Civil Rights movement to fully take effect in the US.

Brown vs the Board of Education

As mentioned earlier, the verdict of Plessy vs Ferguson in 1896 allowed for separate facilities for Blacks and whites as long as they were 'separate but equal'. By the 1950's the NAACP (National Association for the Advancement of Colored Peoples) had filed lawsuits on behalf of Black Americans against various boards of education across the South, the most famous of which being Brown vs the Board of Education, beginning in 1951 and ending in 1954.

The plaintiff, named Oliver Brown, filed a complaint against the board of education in Topeka, Kansas after his daughter, Linda was denied entrance to a whites-only school. He claimed that schools for Black children were not equal to that of white schools, violating the law coming from Plessy vs Ferguson, and that segregation violated the 'Equal protection clause' of the 14th amendment, which asserts that no state is allowed to "deny to any person within its jurisdiction the equal protection of the laws."

The case eventually went before the district court

in Kansas. They ruled that public-school segregation had a 'detrimental effect upon colored children' and contributed to 'a sense of inferiority'; however, they still upheld the 'separate but equal' doctrine.

Brown's case eventually came to the US supreme court, along with four other cases related to school segregation in 1952. These cases were combined into one, becoming known as Brown vs the Board of Education of Topeka.

Thurgood Marshall (who would eventually become the first Black US supreme court justice) represented the plaintiffs in this case. At the time he was the head of the NAACP Legal Defense and Educational Fund.

The case stayed in court for 2 years before they finally came to a unanimous verdict: segregation in schools was illegal. Chief Justice Earl Warren wrote that 'in the field of public education the doctrine of 'separate but equal' has no place,' and that segregated schools were inherently unequal.

Rosa Parks

On December 1st of 1955, Rosa Parks got on a bus home after work in Montgomery, Alabama. The buses were segregated, with Blacks sitting at the back and whites at the front. When a white man got on the bus and couldn't find a seat in the whites-only area, the bus driver asked Parks and three other Black passengers to give up their seats, Parks refused and was subsequently arrested.

Many were outraged at the news of her arrest and as a result the Montgomery Improvement Association (MIA) was formed. This was led by Martin Luther King Jr, a role which placed him at the front of the Civil Rights movement. It was at this point that the movement began to properly gain momentum.

One of the first things that the MIA did was to stage the Montgomery Bus Boycotts, which lasted for over a year and ended with the supreme court ruling segregated seating unlawful on November 14th, 1956.

The Little Rock Nine

In 1957, following the ruling of Brown vs the Board of Education, Central High School in Little Rock, Arkansas asked for volunteers from all-Black high schools to attend the formerly segregated school.

On September 3rd, 1957, nine Black students arrived at Little Rock to begin classes. Upon arrival they were met with a large mob of students and other protesters as well as the national guard. They didn't enter the school.

A few weeks later, the Little Rock Nine tried again to enter the school and succeeded; however, they had to leave shortly after when violence ensued. Finally, after the intervention of President Eisenhower, the Little Rock Nine were escorted to classes by federal troops. They still faced continual prejudice, but were allowed to attend classes and receive an education.

Their efforts brought much-needed attention to the issue of desegregation and began protests on both sides of the 'debate'.

The Civil Rights act of 1957

By 1957, all Americans technically had the right to vote. *Technically*. The Southern states made it more difficult for Black citizens, requiring them to pass the aforementioned impossible literacy tests in order to vote.

President Eisenhower wanted to show commitment to Civil Rights and to minimize racial tension. In order to achieve this, he pressured Congress to consider new Civil Rights legislation.

In September of 1957, the Civil Rights Act was signed. It was the first major Civil Rights advancement since the Post-Civil War Reconstruction and created equal opportunity for *all* voters. It aimed to prosecute anyone who would prevent citizens from voting and investigate voter fraud.

The Freedom Riders

In the 1960 Boynton vs Virginia case, the Supreme Court ruled that segregation in interstate transportation facilities was unconstitutional. Following this, thirteen 'Freedom Riders' consisting of seven Black and six white activists got on a Greyhound bus in Washington DC on May 4th, 1961. They embarked on a bus tour of the American South to protest segregation in bus terminals.

The 'Freedom Riders' drew attention worldwide after experiencing violence from both police officers who were supposed to be upholding the law and from white protesters. On Mother's Day 1961, as the Freedom Riders reached Anniston, Alabama, a mob mounted the bus and threw a bomb into it. The Freedom Riders managed to escape the bus with their lives, but were badly beaten afterwards. The group could not find a driver who was willing to take them any further after that incident.

Attorney General Robert Kennedy negotiated with the Governor of Alabama to find a suitable driver for them, and on May 20th the Freedom Riders continued their journey under police escort. The officers left the bus after it reached Montgomery, where the group was subsequently attacked by an angry mob.

Martin Luther King spoke out about the events and Attorney General Kennedy then sent Federal Marshals to Montgomery to alleviate the issue, since the police were evidently *useless*.

Eventually the Freedom Riders reached Jackson, Mississippi where they were met with many supporters. They were then arrested for trespassing in a white-only facility and sentenced to 30 days in jail. Attorneys for the NAACP brought the case to the attention of the Supreme Court, who repealed the conviction. Hundreds of new Freedom Riders were drawn to the cause, and the rides continued.

Finally, in the autumn of 1961, the interstate commerce commission issued regulations prohibiting segregation in interstate transit terminals. Took 'em long enough, right?

The March on Washington

One of the most famous and well-known events throughout the Civil Rights movement was the 1963 march on Washington. It was organised and attended by Civil Rights leaders such as A. Philip Randolph, Bayard Rustin and Martin Luther King Jr.

More than 200,000 people attended the march. The crowd itself was diverse, with many people coming from different races and backgrounds across America. It was headlined by King's famous 'I have a dream speech', which rapidly became the slogan for equality and freedom worldwide.

The Civil Rights act of 1964

On July 2nd, 1964, president Lyndon B. Johnson signed the Civil Rights Act, legislation enacted by president Kennedy before his assassination in November 1963.

The signing was witnessed by King and other prominent Civil Rights activists. On paper at last, it guaranteed equal employment for all; allowed federal authorities to ensure public facilities were integrated; and limited - but did not stop - the use of voter literacy tests.

Bloody Sunday, 1965

For most of my fellow Brits, Bloody Sunday is an event that occurred in Ireland in 1972 during The Troubles, resulting in the deaths of 14 people. A lot of us may be surprised to learn that the US had their own bloody Sunday, 7 years before.

On March 7th, 1965, 600 peaceful protesters took part in a march from Selma to Montgomery, Alabama, to protest the killing of Civil Rights activist Jimmie Lee Jackson by a white police officer. The march was to encourage *enforcement* of the 15th amendment of the constitution.

Alabama state and local police blocked the protesters from going any further as they approached the Edmund Pettus Bridge. These officers were sent by Alabama governor George C. Wallace, who was a very vocal opponent of desegregation. The protesters refused to stand down and marched forward. In return, they were met with brutal violence. They were beaten, teargassed, and shot at by police. Dozens of protesters were hospitalised, but thankfully none died.

The entire incident was televised; seen across the US, and became known as Bloody Sunday. Many activists rightfully wanted to respond with force, but were talked out of it by Martin Luther King Jr, who would later secure Federal protection for further peaceful protests.

The Voting Rights Act of 1965

After being re-elected in 1964, president Johnson signed into law the Voting Rights Act, making all voter literacy tests illegal. The Act also provided Federal examiners in certain voting jurisdictions and allowed the attorney general to contest local/state poll taxes. As a result, poll taxes were later declared unconstitutional in Harper v. Virginia State Board of Elections in 1966.

The Assassinations of Martin Luther King Jr and Malcolm X

The Civil Rights Movement did a lot of good for Black citizens throughout the US. It didn't do as much for its most prominent organisers. In 1965, Malcolm X (former Nation of Islam leader and founder of the Organization of Afro-American Unity) was assassinated at a rally. Surprisingly, this was not done by white supremacists, but by rival Black Muslims who were opposed to X's newfound ideas that racism, not the white man, was the greatest problem Black Americans faced. Essentially, Malcolm X was killed because he pushed for racial unity over separation.

On April 4, 1968, Civil Rights leader and Nobel Peace Prize recipient Martin Luther King Jr. was assassinated on his hotel room's balcony. It may surprise you to know that King wasn't the widely loved figure that many people believe him to be. In fact, he was considered by many (primarily whites) to be the most hated man in America, having been the victim of multiple failed assassination attempts prior to 1968.

Following King's assassination, huge amounts of emotionally charged riots and protests followed, putting even more pressure on the Johnson administration to push through further Civil Rights laws.

The Fair Housing Act of 1968

The Fair Housing Act came into law days after the
assassination of King, and prevented discrimination in
housing based on race, sex, national origin, and religion. It
did not do anything to undo the harmful effects of
redlining.

Post-Civil Rights Act and the Rodney King
Beatings

Many believe systematic racism ended in the US after the
Civil Rights Act. After all, Black citizens could now buy
property, vote and get married to their white counterparts
without fear of discrimination from the government.

However, systematic racism is still a problem. One
of the largest issues faced by Black Americans following
the signing of the Civil Rights Act is police brutality, and
it's still an issue today.

One of the most famous examples of this is the
Rodney King beating in 1991. King, with his two friends
Bryant Allen and Freddie Helms, were driving in the San
Fernando valley of Los Angeles. King was caught speeding
by police and refused to pull over, leading to a high-speed
chase. They reached speeds as high as 117 mph, eventually
ending after King was cornered by 5 police cars.

King and the others were pulled out of the car and
beaten, King more viciously than the others. Police claimed
that King was reaching for a weapon, even though he was
later found to be unarmed. They claimed he was high at the
time, even though his toxicology report came back

negative. They even claimed that he was resisting arrest, even though the video taken by another citizen showed he stopped resisting after initially being thrown to the ground. The video of the beating went 'viral' (and became so emblematic of police brutality it was later used in a Michael Jackson music video). The offending officers were charged with assault and use of excessive force, but all apart from one were later acquitted.

Police brutality continues to be a problem even today, with an ever-growing list of Black Americans being wrongfully beaten and even killed by officers who are almost never prosecuted due to police unions and qualified immunity (and if you don't know what that is, you need to look it up). Citizens effected are sometimes as young as 5 years old, and never deserve their lives to be threatened in such a brutal manner, whether they have committed crimes or not.

Throughout this essay, we've looked at a lot of history. Only it isn't history, because it's clearly still happening today- we may have put in new labels and legislation, but we haven't changed the thinking that led to racism in the first place. Look no further than the 2020 Black Lives Matter protests in response to the murders of George Floyd and Breonna Taylor.

Floyd was murdered by police after allegedly using fake bills at a store. He was pinned down and suffocated for almost 9 minutes, the whole time saying that he was unable to breathe. It was all caught on video and seen around the world; making all of humanity a witness to his murder. He died of asphyxiation, although the official autopsy implies otherwise; essentially saying that it was his own fault for not being healthy enough to be suffocated for 9 minutes.

Breonna Taylor was a nurse on the front lines, fighting the COVID-19 Pandemic. She was asleep in her own home when police broke in with a no-knock warrant, shooting her multiple times before realising that she wasn't the suspect they were looking for. The suspect in question had been apprehended earlier that day by a different precinct. As of the writing of this text, no officers have been arrested for Breonna's murder, despite public outcry from millions of people.

Throughout the BLM protests, there is one thing that can't be argued: the exact same issues that we were protesting against 55 years ago are still problematic today, but on a much larger, subtler scale. The US government didn't care about their Black citizens 55 years ago and have shown through their deliberate inaction that they *still* don't care now. This is bigger than a racist president, or any racist individual; this is a political system that has been benefiting from and perpetuating the subjugation of Black people for centuries. The timeline I've covered here is only a speck of sand in the hourglass of racist history. It's time we all made a concerted effort to change ourselves, change the system, and change the actions and thoughts that lead to racism and discrimination.

Toys Dream of a Better Tomorrow

By Ruth Thompson

There is no art in the world anymore. There is no love in the world anymore. There is no justice in the world anymore. The world is jerking off to the thought of autonomy, vaping the lost words of running mouths, verbal stipulation, reading the lines over and over again. Pain, so much pain suffocates the world. The media vomits words onto the screen, an unclean scene of bigoted routine. America is violence, politics is violence, police are violence, people are violence, children are becoming violence.

But the one thing which haunts the most:

Who do you call when the murderer wears a badge?

I am white. And I have had my fair share of pain. At some points, I wished life to end because the trauma became too much. 'Why me?' I asked myself countless times. 'My life is doomed my life is shit.' But it took me a while to admit, compared to some, I was doing pretty great. Because I could walk down the street with my hands in my pocket and play with toy guns in my garden and wear a hoodie and stay out late and touch things in a store and argue with my friends over something so minor and forget my ID and have my music loud and… get arrested without getting murdered.

I was privileged. I am privileged. I will always be privileged.

I grew up wanting to move to another country.

"Why?" Grandma asked? "Why would you want to be around immigrants and Black people? You are British for heaven's sake.''

Well first of all, I would be an immigrant, but I guess it's aesthetically pleasing and 'hipster' for a white person to move to paradise? There is some sort of 'expat living the good life' vibe for us, but for them, they are aliens, illegal, immigrants. *I am one of the lucky ones*, I thought. Because the color of my skin gives me opportunity, happiness, freedom, life. And it pains me to say all that, because life shouldn't be like this.

They say you learn from your family growing up. Children copy their parents, it's imperative in primary socialization and it is inevitable children adapt to their surroundings. But it is later in life which matters. You either take their values or you don't, and that, that is everything. I chose to make my own mind up. People around me did what they wanted and said what they wanted, and I always corrected them and always stuck up for those of minority (and will continue doing to this day), but people are stuck in ruts when it comes to bigotry and racism, so I shut them from my life. And that's when I came to realize: I don't have enough middle fingers for this world anymore.

The day the toys started talking was when he was killed. Mum didn't tell me to throw them away because of that. She said I was getting too old for teddys and dolls and I should engage with something more sophisticated. So, I hid a select few and threw the rest into a garbage bag and took them to the charity shop.

***

Later that night, when my eyes were closed, and the world was quiet and dim…

'He deserved it.'

'He was probably armed with a gun. Those Black dudes always carry guns.'

'Like, they say he mis-changed a customer by one pound. I recon he was trying to steal from her and then shoot her. Good on the police for shooting him first.'

'This is boring now. Who cares about them! Hey, Blondie.' Dolly Dave shouted. 'Wanna go for a ride?'

'Can I jump in?' Shouted Action Dude.

'Sure.' Blondie replied. 'Get the music loud, windows down, and drive fast.'

'What about me?' Shouted a muffled voice. No reply. 'Hey, I'm here. In here. It's me. Black Blurbie. Someone gonna help me or?'

The voice was coming from the trash can. Blondie, Dolly Dave, and Action Dude walked over to the bin and stood over it. Mute. Lifeless. Staring. Watching. Empty faces. Empty souls. Empty mouthed.

'I thought he was dead!?' Shouted Dolly Dave. He turned to Action Dude. 'You were supposed to have killed him. He was looking up Blondies skirt! What sort of cop are you?'

'I didn't do anything!? Can't I just come for a ride?' A pain rippled through Black Blurbie's voice.

'Are you going to say it or should I?' Action Dude turned to Blondie. Blondie nodded to Action Dude…

'No. You can't come!'

'But… why?' Black Blurbic flicked a piece of gum from his hair.

'Because the police will stop us and it'll ruin my day.' Blondie rolled her eyes.

'Blondie said all Black people are drug dealers. Sorry, I don't want to get involved.' Dolly Dave said.

'Wait a minute, let me get out.' Black Blurbie pulled his body up with every ounce of strength he held. He dusted himself off. 'You guys are lucky...'

'Here we go, self-deprecation.' Yawned Action Dude. 'Let me tell you a story:'

'My mother said my skin was a beautiful color of custard-cream and my muscles could slice a woman's clit apart and my face could break every genders heart and when I went to school I told them I was manufactured this way and how could you change what you was brought up to be?

And I was told to be better than you, stronger than you, nicer than you. Because I am white and this is our kingdom.

And what I really want to say is you wish you were me because you will never be better than me! I have a gun. I work for the army, and the police, and the secret service. Today I am a cop. Do you really want to get on the wrong side of me?'

Black Blurbie shook his head- 'You know. Racism is so outdated now.'

'I ain't racist.' Said Dolly Dave. 'I love Black Culture. I love Kanye, and Beyonce, and Marvin Gaye. And I read a piece of Black literature the other day. It was cool. Hey, I got away with a crime once.' Dolly Dave turned to Black Blurbie.

'I came home late one night after fucking your mother your brother your lover

Gave them countless orgasms like a defibrillator on their heart their lady parts. They loved it begged for it... she wanted it, her and her Black skin

And she told me it was rape and I said it wasn't because she asked for it-

slut.

And I outrun the police for a while and when they stopped me I blamed her and said she forced it on me and they pinned her down and I watched her scream and cry

blood so much blood blood gushing from her

and they took her and they comforted me while I cried crocodile tears and they sent me for trauma counselling and then I went home and listened to Kanye to relax me.

So yeah, I'm not racist. Kanye is a bro.'

'And I wasn't born racist.' Said Blondie.

'I was walking alone through New York City that day. It was raining hard and I was hard because I saw him walking in the rain. And my parents were racist and didn't understand.

And I brought him home to stay the night and my parents dragged me into the room and told me I had an illness, a sickness, no man's business bringing him into their home. Apparently, girls like me were supposed to marry a six foot eight normal weight white man called Nate.

I told him he had to go and he asked why, and he refused to leave, so I told him why because I didn't want to spend my night in a constant cry.

'Your daughter loves every inch of me so why can't you?' He shouted to my daddy when he was leaving.

And after that, I met Dolly Dave and I love my daddy, he has really made me into a good person.'

And that is when I woke… 'But you aren't a good person. None of you are. I have been listening for a long time.'

'You threw him in the bin.' Blondie stated cockily.

'Because he is ripped. I didn't even question the color of his skin or his cultural background or if he was carrying drugs.' I turned to Black Blurbie. 'Are you okay? How did it happen?'

'I wake up in the morning and I cant believe I have to face the horror of another fucking day. The sun has an optimistic smile and I have a pessimistic sense of exile.

Solitude.

I meander to the supermarket because I run out of sugar and coffee on its own is bitter

And when I get there, there are four women scrolling twitter

And one asked me if I was going to bomb them and one told me to go back to my own country and one asked if I had a gun and one pulled out a gun

Protection she said... this is America.

And I live here born here work here pay tax here pay their benefits here probably die here

And its people like them who make me fear

So I grabbed my sugar and rushed out the door and there they was because they had called the police on me

This is America

And they told me to get down and hold my hands up so I dropped my sugar and held them up and they slammed me into the bin and I felt my rib crack and rotten banana seep into my lungs

Aspiration pneumonia

The smell of ammonia

The stench of corona

And I wanted to shout 'you're hurting me' but mother always told me to keep quiet and do what they say no matter how scared you are because you are Black son, and you need to be quiet in a world full of racists…

A teardrop fell to the floor and they slapped me and put a gun to my head and called me a crybaby

This is america

Black flowers blossom… not here. We are in America.

. My heart hurts my legs hurt my arms hurt my head hurts. I work all day and work all night into the light and into midnight and you all treat me like a harvest mite, parasite. I have no voice, no choice, no reason to rejoice.

I have a heart.

They see me walking and they presume I have a gun

They see me riding and presume I am going to deal

They see me jogging and presume I running from a crime

They see me shopping and presume I stole

They see my skin and shoot.

The dead are listening, the dead are poor, you are listening, my children are crying my children are dying.

This is why I am hurt. He did it to me. The one in the police uniform.' Black Blurbie pointed to Action Dude.

'No one likes a Black grass.' Action Dude pulled the gun from his trousers.

'I am done fighting. I am done being quiet. Do what you need to do.' Black Blurbie knelt down.

'Put the gun away NOW! Before I snap your neck.' I pulled a needle and thread from the drawer and turned to Black Blurbie. 'I can help you.'

'If you touch him, I will leave and never come back. And I am your favorite.' Blondie protested.

'Yeah, and we will go too, won't we, Dolly Dave.' Dolly Dave nodded in sync with Action Dude.

I couldn't help but laugh at them. 'Racism is small dick energy. Go. Now. Never come back.'

Action Dude laughed. 'What are you going to do? Riot?'

'Riots are stupid!' Blondie sniggered.

'Actually, the first Pride was a riot. Women got rights to vote because of rioting. Riots work. Check the history books.' I picked a book of History up and lobbed it at Blondies head. 'Take this for the ride. Goodbye.'

'But… where do we go?' Dolly Dave stuttered.

'I don't care. Anywhere.'

'You will choose… him… over us?' Scoffed Action Dude.

'We all breathe the same air, we all have the same organs. And if you do not support the Black Lives Matter movement, then I say this in the most disrespectful way possible- *we are not friends.*'

'All lives matter, you silly girl.' Said Blondie.

'Breast Cancer.' I replied.

'My mother died from it. It is an organization close to my heart so think carefully about what you say next.'

In the cockiest tone I could manage, I replied, 'All cancers matter…'

Blondie stood, thinking for a moment. 'You'll regret this.'

'No, you'll regret this.'

Part 2

Sue's Head

By S. Collins

Of the two identities in Sue's head, it was often difficult to tell who was the victor.

The Scientist made her fall in love with the universe, the swirls of star-spawn that birthed all forms of organic life. Dad adored the Scientist in Sue. It reminded him of himself. It made him hope maybe Sue could have a better life than he'd managed to carve for himself as an English teacher.

'I'm so glad you decided to study physics, rather than some Shakespeare tripe,' he said, as if he knew about the other voice in her head.

'Oh, so am I,' said Sue, just a little bit too enthusiastic.

The Poet was quiet, but encouraging. Words were there for her in the darkest days, as well as the cloudless climes and starry skies that formed every aspect of her life. This part of her was evasive, keeping silent in the daytime when the Scientist kept her life in order. Her father never considered the Poet a powerful figure in Sue's mind.

Every now and again, after her parents had gone to bed, Sue turned her bedside light on and grabbed her secret notebook. It was purple, plain, and smelled of spilt coffee. The edges of most pages were stained with caffeine and ideas she couldn't bring herself to share with anyone. The Poet within her was usually confined to the subconscious, feeling his way around in the darkness. He shaped the girl's dreams and enticed her to draw squiggly words in the margins of her textbooks. At night, however, words tended to seep from Sue's mind, escaping onto paper in a mass exodus of thought.

As exams drew near, the likelihood of these words doing her any good dwindled. What good could metaphors and beautiful imagery possibly be, when science was the real thing? Sue decided to place her secret notebook back under her pillow, unopened. Instead, she began to read a book by Michio Kaku- *The Inventions that will Transform our Lives*. She hoped one day there would be a machine that could suck the Poet out of her. She could keep him in a little glass case beneath the bed, where he couldn't interfere with her life anymore.

She wanted to be interested in Kaku, but (not for the first time) she found it impossible. *Hmm.* She tried Feynman. Cox. Hawking. *Nothing.* Her heart beat against her ribs, frustrated, as though it wanted to break out of her body. She threw the physics books to the other side of the room.

Come on. Dad needs me to be his little physicist. You need to let go of these childish ideas. Why can't you just be an adult?

Sue looked back at her bookshelf. There was the beat-up anthology of poetry her parents had bought her for school. It cost two pennies- it wasn't worth buying new; not like her physics books.

Before Sue knew it, she was snorting line after line of Byron, O'Hara, Pound, and many more. The rush of it all shot to her brain and begin to buzz. The magical words dissolved into her blood, setting it on fire, re-constructing the cold calculations of her scientific universe.

I have to write this down. Just for a minute.

For a few hours, her hand flew across the page, painting it with a kaleidoscope of thoughts, feelings, and desires Sue didn't want to admit existed within her. Words splattered the page like flower petals, coming together to form a portrait of who she *really* was—not someone her parents would have recognised. Her hands were stained with ink from the rushed writing of so many words. Breath came in heavy gasps. Sue's body shook with an emotion she'd tried to suppress, at least when it came to the arts-- there was no time for childish things, not when she had a future to look out for.

The next morning, the Scientist knew something had gone horribly wrong. He had left the Master clutching books about quantum theory, practical mechanics, Richard Feynman—books designed to make her a prodigy, the girl her parents needed. Someone who could go to university, come back, and buy them a house in a neighbourhood with no bars on the windows. A Poet would be just another empty mouthed layabout.

It seemed she'd been up all night. The Masters hair stuck up in odd places, eyes drooping over deep purple bags, her hand moving as if possessed by Shakespeare himself.

The Poet was still awake.

Only a knock at her door stopped Sues frenzied writing. She looked at her alarm and cursed under her breath. Seven in the morning. Time for school.

Sue looked down at the endless scrawl below her. Her stomach churned the way it had when she'd stolen a book from the school library. Tears came to her eyes, just as they had when her mother had found *Matilda*, by Roald Dahl under her bed and raged. *What's this? Where'd you get this? You know he was a bad man. We don't read this kind of trash in our house.* Sue winced at the memory, running her hands over her own writing. This was the kind of forbidden passion they wrote about in books–books she wasn't meant to have time to read, between studying physics and sleeping.

Sue couldn't make eye contact with Dad on the drive. Instead, she fiddled with the bottom of her too-small jumper. He was trying to have the usual conversation with her.

'You'll probably be able to go to uni for free, at this rate! The Curie Trust sent us another email. They'll give you a full scholarship if you can pass their advanced exam. Room and board included. So, just keep reading your books. Don't worry about how much they cost–it's worth it to see my little girl happy.'

Sue blinked back tears. In these moments, talking to her father was like being under the ocean. Thousands and thousands of tonnes pressing down on her, easing her into cold darkness.

'Yes, Dad.'

'How was the new one? It's on cosmology, right? Is it cool?'

'I guess so.' She pulled a stray thread at the bottom of her jumper and winced as it began to unravel. 'When the

universe was one trillionth of a second old, it was around
the size of a garden pea, but with the mass of everything in
the universe. That's kinda cool.'

She was 16; hardly a child. She'd already picked
out her choices for college, what she'd be studying, where
she'd be living in five years.... None of it relied on words,
unless those words were *Gosh, I just love physics so much*.
Sue just had to hammer her mind into shape. Maths.
Physics. Chemistry. It used to be so easy. She used to spend
hours holed up in a veritable fort of science books. Now
she could barely look at them.

In the library, Sue usually spent lunch poring over
her studies; learning advanced formulae, working tirelessly
to get her hands on the scholarship. Today, however,
something pulled her towards the works of Shelley and
Keats. The words took her far away from the library, to
antique lands where lone and level sands stretched on for
miles, where it must be impossible to feel underwater...

Her lunch, and several physics books, lay forgotten
on the table. *What am I doing?* Nothing answered her but
the pages of endless nonsense-rhymes. But she wanted to
listen to what they had to say.

Not long after that, Sue began breaking into cold sweats in
science class. It wasn't that she no longer felt pulled to the
subject. How could she not be interested in the universe?
No, this was far worse. She couldn't understand a word her
teacher was saying. Her inner monologue played over and
over:

I can't do this. I can't do this. I don't even understand 3D trigonometry. How am I going to understand particle physics? I can't let my dad down. Imagine if he found out about my poems. It would ruin everything! I can't do this.

The short walk to English class was punctuated by enthusiasm and apprehension, resulting in thoughts which echoed around her head.

I've been getting worse at the exams. Maybe I'm just getting sick. I hope I'm just getting sick. If I'm getting sick then I can get better. If I'm not...

'Reputation, reputation, reputation!' Mrs. Carroway interrupted. 'What did Shakespeare mean when he wrote those three words? Was he just having a stroke? Of course not. So, why the repetition, repetition, repetition?'

Sue wanted to raise her hand. *Imagine Dad's face if he found out you know the answer.* Sue made awkward eye contact with Mrs. Carroway before quickly ducking her head down, heart beating out of her chest.

Sue's room at home was white. She hated it, but her mother insisted it looked cleaner that way. It was like living in a clinic, apart from the carpet, which was black and white stripes. It looked like a bar code for giants, but her mother insisted it looked modern and brought a touch of class to the room. And it was the best they could afford, so Sue should stop complaining.

Sue lay on her back, staring at the plain white ceiling of the room. She imagined one day buying a whole set of colours, painting it all sorts of psychedelic patterns. The Scientist would hate it. *Good.*

Sue had three weeks before the advanced exams. At first, everything seemed fine. Then it turned into a monstrous month of scribbling lines Sue thought sounded cool in the margins of her trigonometry notebooks. At least, when she wasn't thinking up haikus concerning thermodynamics, composing sonnets that were half poetry and half algebra, and generally driving both the Poet and the Scientist mad.

When Sue woke up for her advanced physics exam, she was ready to cry. She'd had three hours of nervous sleep, tossing back and forth between awake and unconscious. She woke several times with her heart pounding as though she were in danger- which she was, of course. Sue could lose her future at any moment, with one wrong answer. That was all it would take.

Her father tried to ease the exam-stress, slapping her on the back as she left the house. 'Just think, after today you'll officially be smartest in the family!'

Sue grinned and waved her good-byes before setting off for school. The wind bit across her ankles. *If I get a good job with physics, maybe I can afford some socks that fit.*

For two whole hours, Sue completely failed to put pen to paper. Every time she tried, something held her back. Every question she read turned to gibberish between her ears. By the time the invigilator called for pencils to be put down, all she could hear was the roaring of blood in her skull, crashing against her brain.

I can't do this anymore. I'm not going to university. Not with the Curie Trust. It's useless. I'm useless. I shouldn't even be here anymore.

Sue said nothing to Dad on the drive home. She didn't have to. Her face told the entire story, and his eyes stuck to the road, knuckles tight on the wheel. Her mother wouldn't be home until late—Sue probably wouldn't have the honour of telling her the news, knowing Dad's habit of sneaky texts. There was a celebratory cake in the fridge nobody felt up to eating when they got home.

Sue sat at the foot of her bed, head on her knees. There'd never been a reason to feel so small- not in sixteen whole years. Two years of being mentored by the Trust, five months of revision... for nothing. No, not just nothing- for her parents to be *disappointed* in her. It would've been better if they were mad. At least then Sue could scream at something.

Inside her mind, the Poet addressed the Scientist.

Hey, maybe there's still something I can do.

Oh, what? Give up? Way ahead of you.

Don't be so melodramatic. Einstein and Tesla were dropouts.

They were geniuses. I can't even calculate the upwards velocity of a hot air balloon.

She threw herself on the bed, face-down. Her arm snaked around to hug the mattress, but instead it brushed against something that stopped all her thoughts.

The notebook.

There was no sense calling it a 'secret' anymore. She opened the book and read through several tear-stained pages, each one a melting pot of different emotion- hope, despair, joy, love. All the things physics had once made her feel.

Come on, Sue. There's something inside your head that needs to come out.

She staggered to her desk, bleary-eyed. She swept the boring physics papers onto the bleak carpet, and picked up her pink pen-- she usually used it for marking her papers, but today that couldn't have been farther from her mind.

Something that takes the best parts of poetry and science.

As Sue wrote, the world collapsed in on her. Not in a bad way, like it had in the exam; this was more like a hug. Everything pressed so close she could feel it, it became a part of her-- it made sense! The Poet's creativity, the Scientist's analysis, the Poet's curiosity, the Scientist's answers...

Something beautiful. Not poetry— the Scientist had no love for that. Instead, a short story flowed onto the page; with all that's best of dark and light mixed into every aspect before her eyes.

Thoughts of the failed exam flew from her mind and into the notebook. Sue found that, once the disappointment was out, it became a distant memory. Less painful. Her hands decided to rip the paper up, along with all the physics practice exams which littered the bedroom floor. The room was transformed into a winter wonderland. Her parents weren't quite sure what to make of it when they heard the maniacal giggling upstairs, but they decided not to interrupt.

When Sue looked in the mirror, there was a massive grin staring back at her. The messed-up eyeliner from her forgotten tears seemed more like a joke, as did Planck's constant on a shredded piece of paper, caught in her hair. Of the two battling sides of her, both were the victor.

She had never looked more herself.

Witch-Hunt

By Cassandra Temple

We came not from the shadows

But from the earth, blood and bone

From the Mother, the Maiden

And the Crone

We were your healers and saviors

With Knowledge worth more than gold

We delivered you children

Saved your ill and your old

We lived not in the shadows

But in the community, unrepentant

We were Scientists and doctors

We were spinsters, independent

We were witches

We aided and cured

Until suddenly our help was scorned,

We were maligned and attacked

We were drowned and crushed and burned.

By old men with lots of power and no remorse

And desires so torturous

By money-hungry Land-grabbers

By the sins of the Virtuous

We watched as the children we delivered called us witches

As communities shut their doors

As the women we had saved called us Devil-worshippers

As the men whose families we created called us Demons
and Whores.

*

Witch-hunt

We were forced into the shadows

But the word stepped with us

And lay dormant for centuries

Changing and treasonous

But now it had returned

Risen from the ashes of the women it slaughtered

The same as the Phoenix of legend

Hunting their daughters

But the word has changed

Flipped through a looking-glass

Yelled out in stadiums

To infect en-masse

What once was the martyrdom of women

Has become the excuse of men

What once was a slaughter of the innocent

Has become the defense of the guilty gent

What once was used by aggressors to attack women who
said No

Has become the justification for the aggressors' ignorance
of No

Witch hunt has changed

But not the word

The meaning,

Attacking those who demand to be heard

It was an evil word then

Used to attack those who murdered women

It is an evil word now

Used to defend those who would silence women

The expression of our suffering has been used

To insult us

To malign us

To attack the abused

But today's witches will not be silenced

And die as our fore-mothers did

Silenced and suffering

Their magic undid

We will speak the words that they could not

Live the lives they could not

Enjoy the freedom they could not

Practice our magic as they could not

You say this is a witch-hunt

Led by vile womanhood

To gain power or money

Smear the reputations of the good

This is a witch-hunt

But not an attack on the Him

This is a witch-hunt

But you aren't the victim

Yet your 'witch-hunt' will come

The anger, the fire

The evil will be cleansed

On society's pyre.

The 'witch-hunt' will arrive

Come what may

Because now we are the hunters

And you are the prey

Black Pearl

By Ava Greene

Shuddering slightly after the Sun sailed

Up, down and desperately away from me

I gazed down at my feet

The tide now receeded

A black pearl, the shining globe left me

Black as the torment of the past

Black and white as it flashed in the fading light

I bent down and picked up the pearl,

As if it were my last

A black pearl to match the Sun's soul

Likely as any likeness ever was,

This pearl saw me as I saw him

Perhaps once, but love never stays

So dark and so flawless in my palm that night

Black as the raven who came to warn us

Warn us away from each other

As if he could prize my beloved from my palm

Destroy us

So misguided was he

Him

Was *I?*

This raven looked upon us with pale jealousy

As the pearl clasped at me

This raven grasped at me

Stole me, stole all hopes of being happy

I saw my beloved pearl gleam

As he dropped, as he fell

As I heard my own siren scream

A summoning bell from his heaven to his hell.

And the raven did smile

Demon talons tearing tighter into me

I saw the gleam forever gone

And closed my eyes.

Socio

By Ava Greene

'Couple miles down the road

You'll find a messed up little cabin

Where a man made his sin

And there's a story to be told

Baby, please don't cry!

Oh baby, please don't die!

Well, it was pretty cold that night.

Snow came raining down

Her car'd stopped, no rescue found

'Till he found her an' tucked her in good and tight

Kisses like fire

So you'd never see it coming

Through a manufactured desire

So you'd never suspect something-

And now you're in love with that sociopath

Now you face his wrath

He's so OCD

I'm all tied up keeping him here

I can't be anywhere but near

And he knows what he does to me.

Heated kisses suddenly go loud

And I see in those eyes- you're so proud.

No, no escape for me.

This is your web of lies

And I, a mere fly,

Could never break free of my ties

So is this forever, baby?

I hope so.

After you, there's nowhere to go

But up.

<u>**Witty Ditty**</u>

By Ava Greene

A boy once looked at a girl and said,

I think you're pretty

The girl smiled back and said,

Is that so?

She thought him quite witty.

<u>**Too Young**</u>

By Ava Greene

I saw him today,

As he grinned.

I shyed away,

Not knowing what to say.

Bailar un Poco

By Ava Greene

Bailar un poco, he says to me.

Bailar? I say, showing a shy tendency.

Un poco, oh, just a small amount!

There's little time, so just *Bailar* with me.

There's too many steps, what if I loose count?

Yet *arriba* rises the music and we are free.

Bailar un poco, the music comes again

Bailar... I trail off, voice a strain

I see so much time for us

In your eyes as we *bailar*.

So much trust...

And every twinkle from our crossed stars.

Bailar un poco... I'm dipped, you trail away

Bailar... I've forgotten all else to say.

It's the twinkling of a star

And you're gone

The song ends

The music fades from our *bailar*

Then goes midnight

And I realise we'd been dancing too long.

Hopeless

By Ava Greene

The moon is full as they meet.

Snow falls

Lands gracefully in her hair

Icy water crashes onto the rocks in diamond droplets

And the flagstones greet them

With friendly pitter-patter

As they walk along.

She's beautiful as he's ever seen

In that shifting, flowing blue dress

Strong as the current

She needs him like this; always has

From the first breath of January

To the final, fumbling gasp of December

Where they stand now, half frozen over

And over again

It was cold when they first met

But he gave her cheeks a warm, welcoming glow

With his eyes alone.

Somewhere down the path is music

As they walk along.

The lonely snow clings to them

Like they cling to each other

It's too cold for anyone else.

He is to her a flame

Only a moth such as her could see him like this

He dances, dashes, crashes along with her

Like childhood all over again

Her laughs and gasps behind him

Dress pulled up to her knees.

He slips and falls with her onto crackling grass

She is appalled and still laughs as he grins against her lips

Catching a snowflake on his tongue

Hair a wiry black mess

She never thought she'd love one

With a crooked nose

Never thought she'd find the hair on his arms

Endearing, protective, handsome

Or the stubble on his upper lip

Simply magnetic

She shivers

And how quickly those arms are around her!

How quickly the stubbled lips are pressed to her cheek

Suppressing those shivers as a borrowed jacket

Eclipses her shoulders

Some would say they then walk home.

They know they always were.

Happily Ever After

By Ava Greene

Plenty of fish in the sea

But I think I prefer it

When there's just you and me

And our waters are clearly lit.

You're my first chance at first love

Perhaps there'll be another

Perhaps push won't come to shove-

I've no need for a greater lover.

Blood Moon

By Celia Hameury

They say strange things happen when there is a blood moon. They say… But of course, I'm a sensible man; I don't believe those things. Well, I *didn't* believe them. Now I'm not so sure.

It all began twenty-three years ago.

"There's a blood moon next week, did you know that, Robert?"

My roommate Andre strolled out of his bedroom, his jacket slung over his shoulder. I scowled at him.

"*Of course* I know there's a blood moon next week."

"Right," Andre clicked his tongue and winked at me. "I forgot, you're doing your thesis on astrology."

"*Astronomy*!"

Andre laughed at me

"Same difference, nerd. You know they say weird stuff happens when there's a blood moon, right?"

"Who says that?"

"I donno, people, I suppose. They say it's a bad omen, that it makes people crazy."

"Well, those who say that are morons. How could a lunar eclipse affect human psychology?"

Andre shrugged and swung open the door.

"I donno, man," He said. "It's just what they say. I'll be back in the morning!"

I rolled my eyes and waved a half-hearted goodbye. That idiot Andre liked to tease me, calling my field of study astrology, rather than astronomy. As though someone sensible and intelligent such as I would study something as silly as astronomy! I shook my head at the very thought and took my instant ramen noodle soup into my bedroom. I had a long night of writing ahead of me and I couldn't afford to be going out gallivanting like Andre.

I awoke suddenly, in my desk chair. My desk light was still on, but my computer monitor had gone black. The sky was dark outside my window. I must have fallen asleep while writing. I stood up groggily. My whole body ached. Served me right for falling asleep in my desk chair. I stumbled towards my bed, still half asleep but I felt my foot catch on something on the floor. I hit the ground before I even knew I was falling. I groaned and hauled myself into a sitting position, massaging my bruised elbow. That's when I noticed it, the thing that had tripped me. It was my blazer. What was it doing on the ground I wondered vaguely. That's when I realized that my blazer wasn't the only thing on the ground: my entire room was strewn with my clothes. My dresser drawers were open and empty. Baffled, I staggered out of my room.

"Andre?" I cried.

My idiot of a roommate was sitting on the couch, a beer bottle in his hand. He grinned at me, clearly still drunk from his outing.

"Oh, you're up already?" He slurred, "It's barely what? Like 5 am right?"

He checked his wrist but was not wearing a watch. I threw my hands in the air in frustration. I was now fully awake and perfectly understood what had happened to my room: Andre had pranked me! And I was furious.

"Andre! What the heck is going on in my room? Why did you throw all my clothes on the ground? Is this your idea of a good practical joke? Because it's not funny at all!"

Despite my last words, Andre started to laugh.

"Oh no that's super funny. But I – I didn't do it, man. You got the wrong guy."

"Well if you didn't do it, who did?" I was already sure it was Andre's doing; all I wanted was a confession. An apology would be too much to hope for, I knew.

"Man, I promise, it wasn't me! I donno who did it. Maybe it was you."

"Why would I through my *own* clothes all over *my* room?"

Andre merely shrugged and replied:

"They say strange things happen when there is a blood moon."

I stormed out of the living room and back to my bedroom to clear up my clothes.

The next few days were uneventful enough that I almost forgot about Andre's stupid prank and his nonsense about the blood moon. I worked on my thesis almost non-stop and got little sleep. It wasn't until the night before the infamous blood moon that I was reminded of it all by a second incident. The evening began like most others, with Andre strolling out of his bedroom with his coat slung over his shoulder, his hair tousled.

"You're going out again?" I asked from the kitchen. I was hoping for another evening of peace to work on my thesis.

"Yeah, me and some buds are getting a drink." He put on his shoes before adding, "You should join us."

I doubted it was a serious invitation, more of a courtesy.

"Nah, not tonight. I have work to do."

"Oh well, another time then."

He opened the door but stopped on the threshold.

"Hey what about tomorrow? It's the blood moon, remember? We're all going down to the beach with some blankets and some beers to watch it. You wanna join?"

"Oh, uh," I mumbled, "I have to do some observation of my own for my thesis, but since I'll be on the beach too, I might join you guys after."

"Sounds good!" With that, Andre was out the door and gone. I sighed and shook my head. Why had I agreed to join him and his friends on the beach? I didn't want to hang out with those drunkards. I returned to my room and got to my writing. Once again, I awoke suddenly. This time, the light was off, and I was lying in bed. I didn't remember going to bed, but these days I had so little sleep that I often forgot those sorts of details. I glanced at the window. The sky was pale grey. It must be very early. I wanted to go back to sleep, but something was bothering me. The remnants of a nightmare tickled the back of my mind. I sat up and yawned. I stood up, but immediately sat back down. Once again, my room was an utter disaster, but this time it wasn't strewn with clothes, but with papers.

"No," I whispered. "no, no, no…"

Even in the darkness, even without looking at them carefully, I knew what these papers were. They were the pages of my many notebooks. The notebooks containing all my celestial observations, all my thesis notes. I stood up again, only to fall to my knees amidst the torn pages of my notebooks. Almost sobbing, I gathered the nearest pages into my hands and stared at them, wondering if I could somehow piece my work back together. But the pages were not only torn from their bindings, they were also covered in red scribbles. For the most part, the red scrawls were undecipherable, but on one page I found the unmistakable shape of a crescent moon and below it the word BLOOD in capital letters. Horrified, I threw the paper to the ground. I ran to Andre's room and pounded on his door. I didn't care how early it was; I was livid. When he didn't answer, I barged in and yanked the blankets from his bed.

"Andre!" I shouted, "This time you went too far!"

Andre tugged on his blankets and moaned sleepily.

"It's like 6 am… why are you awake?"

"My notebooks, Andre? My clothes were one thing! But my notebooks… It's too far!"

"Wh-what are you talking about, Robert?"

Seething, I grabbed Andre's arm and dragged him out of his bed and into my room to show him the mess he had made.

"This is what I'm talking about," I shouted. "This… this prank, Andre! This it too far! This was my life's work! It's not funny!"

This time, Andre did not laugh. Instead, he looked at me with something almost like fear in his eyes.

"L-look man," he said shakily, "I swear I didn't do this. I'd never tear up your books, I promise."

"If you didn't do it, who did?"

Andre simply shook his head and murmured:

"They say strange things happen when there is a blood moon."

By the next evening, I had cleared up my room and mostly put my notebooks back together. I was still seething, however, and was therefore glad that Andre didn't talk to me before leaving the apartment. I packed my largest telescope in a long cylindrical bag and slung it over my shoulder. I left our place and headed for the beach, not two blocks away. By the time I got there, many groups of young people had set up camp along the beach. I picked a mostly secluded spot and laid down my blanket. Then I set up my telescope. I heard laughter and singing from the group of people nearest to me, even though they were too far for me to make out more than their silhouettes. I recognized Andre's voice among them. *Great*, I thought, somehow the nearest group of people included the one person I really did not want to see tonight.

For the rest of the night, I did my best to ignore Andre and his rowdy friends as they lit a camp fire, played music and drank heartily. I sat on my blanket, clutching my notebook, waiting for the upcoming eclipse. At last, I saw the reddish light of the blood moon. I grabbed my telescope and focused on the low-hanging, scarlet orb. It was mesmerizing and brilliant, and I could hardly tear my eyes away to jot down the details of my observation.

I don't know at what point it happened, but I must have fallen asleep there, because I awoke to find myself still on the beach. Except I wasn't alone. Andre was lying next to me. I figured he must have come over to talk to me, but found me asleep and decided to join me. But something felt off. Strange.

"Hey, Andre," I whispered. "What are you doing here?"

But Andre didn't wake. Or even move.

"Andre?"

I moved closer and kicked him gently with my foot. Still no movement. I was getting a little nervous now that he may have passed out from all the alcohol he had no doubt consumed. I kicked him a little harder, then reached down and shook him violently. I pulled my hands away suddenly when I noticed the blood in his hair.

"Andre! Come on Andre, get up now. This is not funny! I don't know if this is a prank again or what, but you'd better get up now."

All the while, I was trying to figure out where the blood had come from. Was it even real blood? I found my telescope in the sand. The lens was broken. Had Andre done that? I lifted it from the ground and saw the deep red stains on the end. More blood. Now Andre was a prankster by nature, but this was by far his most elaborate scheme.

"Andre!" I cried brandishing the bloodied telescope at him. "Get up now! If this is a prank, you've gone too far again. So please get up." In the crimson light of the lunar eclipse, my hands looked as red as the blood in Andre's hair.

They say strange things happen when there is a blood moon. Now I don't know if that's true. What I do know is that Andre did not get up. I know that by the time they found his body on that beach, I was somewhere far away. I know that I needn't have worried about my torn notebooks because I abandoned my thesis anyway. And I know that every time there is a blood moon, I lock myself in my bedroom, with the curtains drawn. Just in case.

<u>Conclusion:</u>

What comes next?

So, you've read everything our writers have to say. Hopefully you've learned a thing or two from the essays, you've enjoyed the artistry of the poems, and by buying this anthology you've helped fight racism- well done, you!

But it doesn't end here. Racism is still out there; we still need to be giving it the attention it deserves as an ongoing human rights atrocity. Just because the social media trends have died down doesn't mean you get to turn a blind eye to what's going on in the world.

What can you do?

Continue supporting Black lives:

Donate independently to the **<u>National Bail Fund Network</u>** and **<u>Know Your Rights Camp</u>**, and other such organisations. You can also donate directly to the families of those who have lost loved ones to police brutality and institutional racism. If you can't donate money, donate time. Seek out anti-racism groups in your area and see what you can do to make your community a better place.

Support Black and Minority-owned businesses. Many Minority business owners are struggling due to the pandemic, but you as a consumer have the power to help, by choosing where you spend your money. Sure, a corporately-owned burger is nice, but what about an independently-owned one, fresh-made instead of mass-produced? Supporting local businesses is often a healthier choice than supporting chain franchises.

Become a Legal Observer- someone who is not a participant in protests, but is there to hold law enforcement officials accountable for what they do throughout a protest. The National Lawyers Guild website offers training for those who are interested in helping to end the unconstitutional disruption and interference by law enforcement that often occurs during protests.

Watch Youtube Videos. No, seriously. If you look on YouTube, there are many 'stream-to-donate' videos that are still up from the weeks of the George Floyd Riots. Watching these videos without skipping the adverts is an easy way of donating to BLM charities without spending a single penny.

Follow Black Community leaders on social media. If you can't afford all the books or see all the movies that project Black voices, you can at least follow some on social media. Black authors, beauty professionals, artists, models, politicians, etc... They're all on social media, so don't swipe past them! Before you can amplify Black voices, you have to hear them.

Educate yourself. We've had it repeated a thousand times throughout this book, so I won't labour the point here. You know what to do, you know reflection needs to be done. Read, write, reflect, have uncomfortable conversations, and grow from them.

Vote, for the love of God; Vote! Racist politicians don't just get awarded power in democracies. We put them there, we can vote them out. Vote for politicians who have the best anti-racist track record, who have an interest in passing real anti-racist legislation, who will act on reform. As an anti-racist, you need your interests represented on a governmental level. If you don't vote, you are not represented. Simple as that.

Similarly, **get in touch with your local politicians** who (whether you voted for them or not) represent you. Encourage policy changes by letting them know *exactly* how you feel about the government's response to racism. Don't stop bothering them until you start to see some goddamn institutional change. Hold them to account, because they are.

Sign petitions for justice when you see them pop up. If you don't see them pop up, seek them out. It doesn't have to be something you do every day or even every week, but maybe every other Sunday you could resign yourself to signing a petition or two and sharing it around.

Set up your own petitions or GoFundMes, if you can. It's time-intensive, but simple enough to do. Facebook even has a way to set up fundraisers in such a way that all profits are donated directly to the nonprofit of your choosing.

Be vocal. Share articles, talk to your friends and family, encourage people to vote for change, and just do what you can in small ways on a daily basis.

Remember, anti-racism is a lifetime of learning, unlearning, and relearning. It's okay to take a break, put down this book, and take a deep breath (maybe eat some muffins) before you carry on fighting the good fight.

Thank you for reading this book.

Helplines:

UK:

Anxiety UK

03444 775 774

www.anxietyuk.org.uk

A charity providing support if you have anxiety.

Bipolar UK

www.bipolaruk.org.uk

A charity helping those with manic depression or bipolar disorder.

CALM

0800 58 58 58

www.thecalmzone.net

The Campaign Against Living Miserably, for men aged 15 to 35.

Crimestoppers
0800 555 111
www.crimestoppers-uk.org
Call anonymously with information about any type of crime.

Equality Advisory & Support (EASS)
0808 800 0082
www.equalityadvisoryservice.com
They can assist you with any issues relating to equality and
human rights across England, Scotland and Wales.

Mind

0300 123 3393

www.mind.org.uk

Promotes the views and needs of people with mental health
problems.

PAPYRUS

HOPELINEUK 0800 068 4141

www.papyrus-uk.org

Young suicide prevention society.

Samaritans

116 123 (free 24-hour helpline)

www.samaritans.org.uk

Confidential support for people experiencing feelings of
distress or despair.

SAMM (Support After Murder and Manslaughter):
0845 872 3440
0121 472 2912
www.samm.org.uk
They provide emotional support for those who have lost
loved ones through murder or manslaughter.

Stop Hate Line:

0800 138 1625
www.stophateuk.org
They provide immediate advice/support to anyone who is a
victim or witness to a hate crime.

SupportLine.org.uk

01708 765200

A confidential telephone service that will provide
emotional support to anyone, about anything. They aim to
help people before they reach the point of crisis. They are
able to support those who have suffered from a wide range
of issues, including: racial harassment, loneliness,
depression, anxiety, anger, and bullying. They are open to
any individual from any age group.

The Monitoring Group:

http://www.tmg-uk.org/about/

020 7582 7438

A leading anti-racist charity, based in London. They aim to improve race relations, educate and raise awareness of racism where it exists, and to relieve the needs of those who are suffering racial violence/harrassment.

Victim Support:
0808 168 9111
www.victimsupport.org.uk
They help people cope with the effects of crime, even if the crime is uninvestigated/unreported. They can also provide information on victim support groups near you.

Victim Support National Hate Crime Report and Support Centre Wales:
0300 3031982
www.reporthate.victimsupport.org.uk
An organisation based particularly around Wales that deals with advocacy, restorative justice, serious injury compensation claims, independent police commissioner complaints, process assistance, and more.

Victim Support Scotland:
0800 160 1985
www.victimsupportsco.org.uk
Helpline for anyone affected by crime, regardless of
whether or not it has been reported.

United States:

In Our Names Network

https://www.inournamesnetwork.com/

They are not just one organisation, but a network of organisations dedicated to documenting sexual violence by law enforcement officers, responding to unmet mental health needs the police can't seem to deal with, developing strategies for police accountability beyond prosecution, and building safety for Black women and Black LGBTQ+ people.

National Hopeline

https://www.imalive.org/

1-800-SUICIDE (1-800-784-2433)

They'll set you up with a crisis counsellor.

National Suicide Prevention Lifeline

https://suicidepreventionlifeline.org/

1-800-273-TALK (1-800-273-8255)

They can direct you to a nearby crisis centre. They also provide 24 hour free and confidential support to those in distress, they'll help you if any of your friends/loved ones are in crisis or they can help you prevent crisis being reached in the first place.

The NAACP:

https://www.naacp.org/

A well-known organisation that works to ensure political, educational, social, and economic equality; particularly to remove the barriers of racial discrimination and raise public awareness of racial discrimination.

Australia:

Beyond Blue

1300 22 4636

https://www.beyondblue.org.au/

Aim: to increase awareness of depression and anxiety and reduce stigma.

Kids Helpline

1800 55 1800

https://kidshelpline.com.au/

A free and confidential counseling service specialising in children and young people ages 5-25.

Lifeline

13 11 14

https://www.lifeline.org.au/

24-hour crisis counselling, support groups and suicide prevention services for many kinds of mental illnesses.

MindSpot

1800 61 44 34 AEST

https://mindspot.org.au/

A free online and telephone service for those living with anxiety, depression, and low mood/stress.

QLife

1800 184 527

https://qlife.org.au/

Provides services to all ages of LGBTQ+ individuals.

Resources:

Websites:

https://Blacklivesmatter.com/

A network working to bring justice, healing, and freedom to Black people worldwide.

https://Blackmaleachievement.org/

CBMA is a network of leaders and organisations working to support Black men and boys.

https://Blacktrans.org

An organisation centred around improving the Black trans experience.

https://centerforBlackequity.org

Information and resources to educate and empower Black LGBTQ+ people in the fight for equality.

www.direct.gov.uk
A UK Government site with information/advice on crime, justice, and legal proceedings.

https://nationalbailout.org/Black-mamas-bail-out/

A Black-led/centred organisation of lawyers and activists working to end pretrial detention systems and mass incarceration.

www.ourwatch.org.uk

Information about Neighbourhood Watch schemes throughout the UK.

www.report-it.org.uk

A UK, police-funded site that helps you deal with all kinds of hate crime and is aimed at improving the services police provide to minority communities.

www.reportharmfulcontent.com

Advice on reporting harmful online content such as bullying, unwanted sexual advances, and violent/suicidal/threatening/pornographic content.

https://tellmamauk.org/

A UK site supporting victims of anti-Muslim hate, which can also help you find support with partner agencies if you have been targeted for being (or even appearing to be) a Muslim.

Books:

Children of Blood and Bones by Tomi Adeyemi

The New Jim Crow: Mass Incarceration in the Age of Colorblindness By Michelle Alexander

Unafraid of the Dark by Rosemary L Bray

I'm Still Here: Black Dignity in a World Made for Whiteness By Austin Channing Brown

Free Cyntoia by Cyntoia Brown-Long

Let's Get Free: A Hip-Hop Theory of Justice by Paul Butler

Unapologetic: A Black, Queer, and Feminist Mandate for Radical Movements By Charlene A. Carruthers

Eloquent Rage: A Black Feminist Discovers Her Superpower By Brittney Cooper

When They Call You a Terrorist: A Black Lives Matter Memoir by Patrisse Khan-Cullors and Asha Bandele

Are Prisons Obsolete? By Angela Y. Davis

Women, Race & Class By Angela Y. Davis

White Fragility by Robin DiAngelo

The Hidden Rules of Race: Barriers to an Inclusive Economy by Andrea Flynn, Susuan R. Holmberg, Dorian T. Warren, and Felicia J. Wong

How Not to Get Shot: And Other Advice From White People By D. L. Hughley and Doug Moe

Waking Up White, and Finding Myself in the Story of Race by Debby Irving

Hood Feminism: Notes From the Women That a Movement Forgot By Mikki Kendall

How to Be an Antiracist by Ibram X. Kendi

Sister Outsider By Audre Lorde

We Want to Do More Than Survive: Abolitionist Teaching and the Pursuit of Educational Freedom By Bettina L. Love

When Chickenheads Come Home to Roost: A Hip-Hop Feminist Breaks It Down By Joan Morgan

Pushout by Monique Morris

Born A Crime by Trevor Noah

Algorithms of Oppression: How Search Engines Reinforce Racism by Safiya Umoja Noble

So You Want to Talk About Race by Ijeoma Oluo

An African American and Latinx History of the United States by Paul Ortiz

Citizen: An American Lyric By Claudia Rankine

Just Mercy by Bryan Stevenson

Why Are All the Black Kids Sitting Together in the Cafeteria? And Other Conversations About Race by Beverly Daniel Tatum

Men We Reaped by Jesmyn Ward

How We Get Free: Black Feminism and the Combahee River Collective by Keeanga Yamahtta-Taylor

Movies:

Fruitvale Station (Directed by Ryan Coogler)

Just Mercy (Directed by Destin Daniel Cretton)

Selma (Directed by Ava DuVernay)

Barry (Directed by Vikram Gandhi)

If Beale Street Could Talk (Directed by Barry Jenkins)

Moonlight (Directed by Barry Jenkins)

Do The Right Thing (Directed by Spike Lee)

I Am Not Your Negro (Directed by Raoul Peck)

Get Out (Directed by Jordan Peele)

Higher Learning (Directed by John Singleton)

The Hate U Give (Directed by George Tillman Jr.)

The Immortal Life of Henrietta Lacks (Directed by George C. Wolfe)

Series:

Dear White People (Netflix)

Pose (FX)

Queen Sugar (OWN)

Self-Made: Inspired by the Life of Madam C. J. Walker (Netflix)

Seven Seconds (Netflix)

Top Boy (Netflix)

When They See Us (Netflix)

Documentaries:

13th (Directed by Ava DuVernay)

Boss: The Black Experience in Business (Directed by Stanley Nelson)

LA92 (Directed by T. J. Martin and Daniel Lindsay)

Owned: A Tale of Two Americas (Directed by Giorgio Angelini)

The Black Power Mixtape 1967-1975 (Directed by Göran Olsson)

The Children's March (Directed by Robert Hudson and Robert Houston)

The Kalief Browder Story (Directed by Jenner Furst)

Welcome to Leith (Directed by Christopher K. Walker and Michael Beach Nichols)

*May we remember each and every
one of these people, who are so
much more than names. May we
never forget:*

Shukri
Abdi

Matthew
Ajibade

Tanisha
Anderson

Ahmaud
Arbery

Anthony
Ashford

Dalian
Atkinson

Aaron
Bailey

La'vante
Biggs

Sandra
Bland

Rumain
Brisbon

Michael
Brown

Paterson
Brown

Nunu
Cardoso

Philando
Castille

Wendell
Celestine

Rashan
Charles

Alexia
Christian

Stephon
Clark

Jamar
Clark

Dominique
Clayton

Julian Cole

Edson Da
Costa

Alonzo
Smith-
Tyree
Crawford

Terence
Crutcher

Smiley
Culture

Michelle
Cusseaux

Jordan
Davis

Christopher
Davis

Albert
Joseph
Davis

Billy Ray
Davis

Brian Kieth
Day

Michael
Lorenzo
Dean

Kobe
Dimock-
Heisler

Samuel
Dubose

Mark
Duggan

Jordan
Edwards

Salvado
Ellswood

Miguel
Espinal

Jonathan
Ferrell

George
Floyd

Jamel
Floyd

Janisha
Fonville

Ezell Ford

Ronell
Foster

Peter
Gaines

Joy
Gardner

Eric
Garner

Brendon
Glenn

Freddie
Gray

Cherry
Groce

Akai
Gurley

Mya Hall

Eric Harris

DJ Henry

Kevin
Hicks

Anthony
Hill

Justin
Howell

Dominic
Hutchinson

William
Chapman
II

Antwon
Rose II

John
Crawford
III

Cynthia
Jarrett

Botham
Jean

Atatiana
Jefferson

Lamontez
Jones

Corey
Jones

Bettie Jones

David
Joseph

Freddie
Carlos
Gray JR.

Keith
Childress
JR.

India
Kager

Felix Kumi

Victor
Manuel
Larosa

Stephen
Lawrence

Quintonio
Legrier

Marco
Loud

Laquan
MacDonald

Asshams
Pharoah
Manley

Joseph
Mann

Michael
Lee
Marshall

Trayvon
Martin

Kevin
Matthews

Christopher
Mccorvey

Tony
McDade

Natasha
Mckenna

Keith
Harrison
McLeod

Mzee
Mohammed
-Daley

Sean
Monterrosa

Jimmy
Mubenga

Belly
Mujinga

Randy
Nelson

Gabriella
Nevarez

Michael
Noel

Paul
O'Neal

Dante
Parker

Richard
Perkins

Dyzhawn
Perkins

Nathaniel
Harris
Picket

Junior
Prosper

Eric
Reason

Sarah Reed

Jerame Reid

Tamir Rice

Tony Robinson

Torrey Robinson

Darius Robinson

Troy Robinson

Calin Roquemore

Aura Rosser

Michael Sabbie

Jonathan Sanders

Walter Scott

Antronie Scott

Demarcus Semer

Frank Smart

Trevor Smith

Sylville Smith

Kionte Spencer

Alton Sterling

Darrius Stewart

Roger Sylvester

Darius Tarver

Breonna Taylor

Christian Taylor

Terrill Thomas

Benni Lee Tignor

Emmett Till

Willie Tillman

Mary Truxillo

Pamela Turner

Phillip White

Christopher Whitfield

Janet Wilson

Alteria Woods

And many more…

Rest in Power

Because in an unjust society,

it is impossible to rest in peace.